New to the Game 3

Malik D. Rice

Lock Down Publications and Ca$h Presents

New to the Game 3

A Novel by *Malik D. Rice*

Malik D. Rice

Lock Down Publications
P.O. Box 944
Stockbridge, Ga 30281

Copyright 2020 by Malik D. Rice
New to the Game 3

Lock Down Publications
Like our page on Facebook: Lock Down Publications @
www.facebook.com/lockdownpublications.ldp
Cover design and layout by: **Dynasty Cover Me**
Book interior design by: **Shawn Walker**
Edited by: **Lashonda Johnson**

Stay Connected with Us!

Text **LOCKDOWN** to 22828 to stay up-to-date with new releases, sneak peaks, contests and more…

Thank you!

Submission Guideline.

Submit the first three chapters of your completed manuscript to ldpsubmissions@gmail.com, subject line: Your book's title. The manuscript must be in a .doc file and sent as an attachment. Document should be in Times New Roman, double spaced and in size 12 font. Also, provide your synopsis and full contact information. If sending multiple submissions, they must each be in a separate email.

Have a story but no way to send it electronically? You can still submit to LDP/Ca$h Presents. Send in the first three chapters, written or typed, of your completed manuscript to:

LDP: Submissions Dept
P.O. Box 944
Stockbridge, Ga 30281

DO NOT send original manuscript. Must be a duplicate.

Provide your synopsis and a cover letter containing your full contact information.

Thanks for considering LDP and Ca$h Presents.

ACKNOWLEDGMENTS

Giving a big thanks to the Higher Power above. I want to acknowledge all my family and friends that's taking part in the construction of this empire being built. I also want to thank all my readers and supporters, you all are also a vital piece of my legacy. My vision is so vivid these days that it's becoming possible for individuals around me to see, and feel, it as well. That's all I ever wanted in life. This may be a career for most, but it's a way of life for me. Just remember that it only gets better. I'm elevating as a person as my storytelling skills do the same. It's my life. It's a beautiful process. It's an exciting journey. It's literally history in the making.

Malik D. Rice

CHAPTER 1

Mooski swerved in-and-out of traffic in his Camaro while his kill team struggled to keep up. He wasn't necessarily trying to lose them. He was just wired up off all the powder he'd shoved up his nostrils. He wasn't worried about crashing, and he wasn't worried about getting pulled over. He was at the point in his life where he honestly wasn't worried about anything. As long as he had his Mafioso stripes, and the sexy girl sitting by his side, he was content.

"Nigga, you need to slow yo' ass down!" Babie advised after snorting a sizable bump of coke straight out of the bag from a straw.

Mooski had turned her out in more ways than one. "Don't be snorting up all my damn shit!"

He reached over trying to snatch the bag away from her, but she pulled it back just out of his reach. "You don't need no damn more! You done did a brick today. You gon' fuck around and overdose, nigga."

"Fuck it." He waved her off with his free hand.

Twenty minutes later, they were in Glenville, Georgia. He had the designated address logged into the GPS and followed the directions all the way there.

"Where the hell we going, anyway?" asked Babie curiously while looking around at the woods on either side of the isolated road.

"Just sit back and ride, bae. You wanted to take this trip with me. Now you're here, so just be easy shawty."

A few minutes later, the GPS spoke over the blasting music instructing them to make the left turn onto a narrow dirt road that seemed to be swallowed up by thick woods. Mooski was glad he decided to take the trip in the daytime because he would've been *very* uneasy with the route in complete darkness. The dirt road opened to a small dirt field where two large RVs were parked right next to each other.

"What the fuck is this all about, bae?" asked Babie while looking at the two puppies on the ground struggling to get to each other from their leashes that were secured to bolts buried in the ground.

"You'll see, come on." He cut the car off and waited for his kill team to get out of their truck, then got out.

A chubby white man who couldn't have been ashamed of his body came out of an RV with nothing but a pair of cut off shorts on. It was uncomfortably hot in the patch of woods, even with the shade from the trees. "How y'all fellers doing this afternoon?" he asked in a deep Southern back wood accent. He scanned the crowd unfazed by all the guns, mugs, and tattoos. He wrestled alligators on a bad day, he wasn't scared of a few teenage thugs.

"You must be, Cable?" Mooski asked while stepping forward leaving Babie and his Mobsters behind.

"The one, and only. Nice to meet you! You must be, Mooski?" he asked with his hand extended for a shake.

Mooski shook his hand. "Yeah. I hear you the man to talk to around these parts?"

"Yeah, it depends on what you trying to buy. My cousin tells me you were interested in fighting dogs, and as you can see, I have two healthy blue nose pitbull puppies right here. Who comes from a *long* line of vicious fighting champions, one male and one female."

Mooski kneeled to get a better look at the puppies. He waved his hand signaling for someone to come over. No one knew exactly who he was trying to summon, so they all stepped forward into the middle of the field.

"Aye, Gutta. What you think?" he asked his best friend without taking his eyes off the puppies who were snarling and growling at them all.

Gutta's uncle fought dogs all his life and was very close to Gutta. If anybody there knew if the dogs were worth purchasing, Gutta was the one. He kneeled next to Mooski studying the dogs through squinted eyes. "Them some real killers right there."

He looked up at Cable. "How much?"

"I'll sell y'all both of 'em for seven thousand."

Mooski flashed his famous mug. "Seven racks?"

"Yeah. Why not? You're guaranteed to win at least a few hundred thousand off these babies."

"Alright, I'm gon' hold you to that now," Mooski warned.

While they talked business, Babie, scanned the premises out of pure boredom. She was more fascinated with the RV than she was with the puppies, so that's where her attention drifted to. She always wanted to rent an RV, and just hit the road like she'd seen in the movies. She was just about to take her attention elsewhere when she caught a glimpse from the sun reflect off a pair of lenses of some sort.

"Who's that in the window?" she asked while pointing at the RV.

A second later, a shot fired from a rifle, and the bullet struck her index-finger knocking it clean off. She dropped to the ground and started screaming hysterically as bullets flew over her head.

***

Just like Toe-Tag predicted, Mrs. Bloomfield ended up being a valuable asset to his camp. Out of everybody that gangbanged her that rememberable night in her living room, Dreek was the only one that still dipped in her honey jar. Of course, she made sure all his bills were paid, so Toe-Tag understood, but the relationship he shared with her was very different.

They were at a small park downtown that was across the street from a Starbucks that Mrs. Bloomfield visited on a regular basis after leaving the gym. She sat on a park bench next to Toe-Tag, giving him the seductive eye.

"What did I tell you the other ten times you tried to throw yourself onto me?" he asked seriously with a straight face.

She rolled her eyes slightly. "You don't want anything to do with the cobwebs in between my legs?"

"And that's not going to change. I didn't call this meeting for that. You still have that property out in Columbus?"

"The house? Yeah. The family that was renting it found a house for sale, so it's still on the market. Why, you trying to rent it?"

Toe-Tag eyed a small group of businessmen passing them on the walkway. "Yeah, I'm about to do some expanding, and the house just-so-happens to be in the perfect location. I'm sure I can count on a nice discount right?"

"What are you willing to do for it?" she asked while giving him a knowing look.

She was a nympho and wanted some of Toe-Tag the worst way. Just by the way he walked and talked, she knew he had what it took to mistreat her properly.

"Not kill you." He got up and left her on the park bench with wet panties as usual.

***

Handsome, and Kamya, shared a decent condo on the nicer side of Moreland Avenue. It was funny that they were only a few short miles away from the hood but felt like they were in a whole different world.

Kamya was in the kitchen cooking breakfast for her man while watching a classic comedy movie on the small flat-screen TV that was embedded in the granite wall. Handsome had that feature added specifically for her.

She hadn't felt this much peace in her short life. She'd been surrounded by drama and pain all her life up until now. It was sad to say, but she came from a very toxic family, and now that she was away from them, life was better for her. She loved Babie and her mother from the bottom of her heart, but Babie was on a different life path than her, and her mother hadn't been seen since Rampage kicked her out of the hood. So, it was her, Handsome, and the unborn child in her stomach from there on out.

The doorbell rang and a bright smile appeared on her face. Her company had finally arrived. No matter how right Handsome started living, he would always be haunted by his past, which meant he would forever be paranoid. So, he only allowed Kamya to have two visitors over the house. Babie and Jasmine, Babie was out of town with Mooski, so she invited Jasmine over for Sunday morning breakfast.

Handsome came rushing into the front room with his AK-74 in one hand with an alert expression on his face.

"It's just Jasmine, babe. Go back in the room and play the game," she insisted with a loving hand on his chest.

He thought about it, but walked past her, and answered the door just to be safe. He opened the door, and it was Jasmine as expected. He waved her inside hurriedly and stuck his head out the door both ways to make sure everything was good before locking the door back and returning to the bedroom after giving Jasmine a nod for a greeting.

Jasmine just shook her head once he was out of sight.

"What?" Kamya asked amusingly.

"That nigga there so damn extra. Anywayyy, what's up girly-girl? How you been?" She gave Kamya a tight hug, then kneeled so she could be leveled with her belly. "And how my goddaughter been?"

Kamya smiled down at her showing all her teeth. She loved when people rubbed her belly. "We been good! Handsome keeps making us go to the doctor's office all the time, though."

"He just being a good father, that's all. How far along are you?"

Kamya looked at her blankly how she usually did when she wasn't comprehending.

"How long have you been pregnant, Mya?" she asked more simply.

"Oh, it's gon' make nine weeks tonight at twelve o'clock. I can't wait for my stomach to get big. When you going to have a baby, Jassy?"

Jasmine stood up. "I already have a baby."

"No, I mean like your own baby that you push out yourself."

"I don't know, girl. Karma still young, and definitely a handful. I'm not really in a rush. But guess what, girl?"

"What?" Kamya asked excitedly, she loved surprises.

"I did find a guy that I'd probably try it with."

Malik D. Rice

CHAPTER 2

Wopp wasn't too big on security, especially not in his own hood. What good was life if he couldn't ride around in his own hood safely without security? It was a decent summer day outside with clear skies, so he opted to take his bright green drop-top Benz out for a spin.

He had one of *T.I.'s* old hit singles *Whatever You Like* playing on the stereo while making his way down Old National boulevard to meet up with one of his younger side pieces. His gas light came on before he got there, so he made a pitstop at a BP gas station.

He wasn't worried about the group of young hoodlums draped in blue that was now staring him down intensely. Everybody on the Southside knew who he was, he was a legend and labeled untouched for the most part. He didn't have to walk inside the store due to the digital purchase systems that were now embedded into most gas pumps throughout the country. He was grateful for that, so he could stay close to the M-16 he had on the backseat. He was labeled untouched, but niggas broke rules every day, and he didn't want to take any chances.

It took him a few minutes to fill his tank and hop back into the car. He tried to burn rubber out of the parking lot but was blocked in by a motorcade of dirt bikes, and ATVs. A familiar face hopped off a blue four-wheeler and made its way toward Wopp's car.

He literally hopped in the passenger's seat like he was invited. "Follow them."

"What?" Wopp looked over at Pooh Bear menacingly.

"What kind of games you playing? I'm not going nowhere, nigga! Get up out my shit!"

"You know me well enough to know I don't play no muthafuckin' games, nigga. I'm right here for a reason. Now follow them like I said," he instructed irritably. He didn't want to be there any more than Wopp wanted him there, but business was business.

A few short minutes later, they were pulling up into Brickfield apartments, a popular loitering spot for the local Crips in the area.

Wopp followed them into the back of the complex where the motorcade of motorbikes surrounded the Benz.

Wopp looked around and took a deep breath. "What's all this about, Bear? I thought we was good."

Pooh Bear started laughing suddenly. He and Diamond favored each other in many ways from the brown-skin to the shiny white teeth. The only difference between them was that he was taller and way crazier. "*Good?* Nigga, we met *one* time. Just because I ain't robbed you yet don't mean we good."

"Do what you think you need to do," Wopp instructed.

"Nigga, if I wanted to do something to you, it would've already been done at the gas station. I got you right here because we got business that needs to be discussed," Pooh Bear informed matter-of-factly.

"I'm listening."

***

It always amazed Kapo how New York could be so cold in the winter, but so hot in the summer. He'd witnessed the best and worst of both seasons and was glad 2-Tall was summoning him up there in the summer this time. He looked down at Mina walking next to him in a sophisticated off-white Christian Louboutin summer dress. Her peach Giovanni heels clacked on the hard, expensive marble floor that covered most of the mansion they were being escorted through.

"You alright?" he asked.

"Of course. Why'd you ask me that?" She hooked her arm through his.

"Because this is a big change of lifestyles for you. I know the life I live can be overwhelming, and I don't want to put too much on your plate."

She shook her head. "I understand what you're getting at, but don't worry about me. I'm grown, and I make my own decisions. You're not putting pressure on me. Plus, I always wanted to see how it would feel to be friends with a Cartel princess."

"Oh, you got jokes? Don't speak too fast," he warned seriously knowing just how psychotic, and overbearing Malina could be.

The butler escorted them to a large dining room where they were met by 2-Tall and Malina who were dressed for the occasion as well.

"I used to have a thing for Asians once before. That phase is over now, but I'm glad you found somebody to hold you down. After all the shit you've been through, you definitely need a crutch, bro," 2-Tall stated matter-of-factly.

They were on the lower level of the seemingly endless mansion. It was more like a castle in the middle of nowhere. A place Malina called home a few months out of every year. There was a massage parlor, a bowling ally, and a few more unusual pleasurable sections throughout the lower level, but the section 2-Tall decided to chill in was the one that blew Kapo's mind away the most.

"How is it possible for tigers and panthers to coexist in the same environment?" he asked amazed at the sight.

They stood behind a huge glass watching the young cubs play in an artificial tropical environment that didn't seem artificial at all.

2-Tall nodded his head in understanding. He understood perfectly why Kapo changed the subject and respected it. Sometimes the best way to deal with demons was not at all. "You'll have to ask the employees that deal with them, but it never ceases to amaze me. This is my favorite site to see in this place. I come down here to get my mind right—get away from all this shit. Get away from Malina's crazy ass."

"It's ironic how millions of men would gladly kill to be in your shoes, but the more time I spend around you, the more it seems like you'd kill to get out of your own shoes."

"Thinking about throwing a pair of lion cubs in there just to see how it'll work." He took a big sip of the exotic liquor in his glass without taking his eyes off the beautiful cubs behind the glass.

Kapo smiled faintly. It was clear that they both had demons they didn't care to deal with or talk about. Maybe it was for the best, or maybe they just needed to learn to trust one another a little more.

Malik D. Rice

CHAPTER 3

"It's been a minute since we been in public like this shawty. I feel weird as fuck, I feel exposed," Monster informed truthfully with an uneasy expression on his bright face.

They dined in the VIP section of Bizzy's, which was still one of Atlanta's most prized upscale restaurants.

"Yeah, me too, but I felt like popping up from the underworld for a lil' bit, and this where I wanted to do it at. You know the first time I ate here I had to finesse the manager to get in this muthafucka," Toe-Tag reminisced.

"Yeah, I remember you telling me some shit like that."

"Crazy how far a young nigga done came in this shit. Anyways, where the fuck is my brother? He supposed to meet us here, too."

"Shit, he probably laid up with Lakisha."

Toe-Tag squinted his eyes with a crumpled face. "Lakisha from the hood? Lil' Quavo's mama?"

"Yuppp! She must've put that pussy on him good because they been glued together for the past week."

Toe-Tag didn't understand. "What the hell make her want to fuck with a street nigga all of a sudden? You know how long niggas in the hood been trying to hit that? Now she wanna fuck with my brother? I don't know, bro."

"Yeah, it is kind of weird, but Mazi a different type of nigga. He probably just hit her with that prison talk."

"I guess."

A brunette waitress walked up to their booth. "Good afternoon gentlemen. What will you be having today?"

Toe-Tag ordered steak and lobster salad for both of them.

"I got word from Mooski that they got in some shit down by Savannah, and Babie ended up getting shot," Monster informed.

"Whattt!" Toe-Tag bellowed drawing nearby attention. "How the fuck?"

"The better question is, why the fuck? They was just down there trying to buy some pitbull puppies that's bred to fight. Ain't like he had her on a mission or nothing."

"Who they went to buy the puppy's from?"

"Some redneck that go by the name Cable. He dead now though. They trying to find the nigga that put them on to the redneck as we speak. Plus, Babie's alright. Her middle finger got shot off, but she'll live."

Toe-Tag shook his head in disappointment. "Make sure she got a full escort back to the hood when they check her out of that hospital and did they transfer AK to Grady yet?"

Monster slapped his head in frustration. "Damn, I forgot bro'."

"Come on, fat boy! I know you got a lot on your plate, but that's what the rest of the Mafioso's is for. If you don't have time to do something, pass the task down."

"I'll get it done man. How the movie shit going?"

"That shit about to put us on the map, big bro'."

***

Back in the hood, Quavo walked into his apartment and his eyes lit up when he saw Mazi sitting on his couch playing his PlayStation 4. "What's good, big bro? Where my mamma at?"

He loved the idea of Mazi messing around with his mother. Before he was just another Mobster in the hood, now he was relevant. He was already getting special treatment around the hood, and he loved it.

"In the room getting ready. I'm about to take her out to this lounge on the Northside," Mazi answered after pausing the game. "Come here, I need to talk to you anyway."

He walked over and sat on the couch next to him.

"Keep it real with me now. How you feel about me fucking with yo' mamma?"

"I mean, it's good. As long as you don't beat on her, or no shit like that, I'm not tripping. She definitely needs a man in her life, though."

Mazi smiled slightly. "Shit, I'm surprised she even fucking with a nigga."

"Me too, but I'm glad though," Quavo admitted.

***

"That boy Mazi don't play. Ain't no way he came home and snatched Lakisha's fine ass," Quay said while watching the new couple get into the brand new 2015 Maserati truck that Toe-Tag bought Mazi.

He sat on the green box on the side of his apartment building with Dreek enjoying the lovely summer weather. They both had just come back from the shooting range with their kill-teams, now they were winding down looking over the hood as the sun made its decline.

"Yeah, he definitely did that. I know lil' Quavo's happy," Dreek said.

"You think he gon' jump up under Mazi?"

Dreek shrugged his shoulders nonchalantly. "I fuck with the lil' nigga, but I really don't give a damn. I got thirteen other Mobsters to look after."

"I feel that. How you been holding up, though? You really been a lil' distant these past few months. What you got up your sleeve?" asked Quay.

"Why a nigga got to have some up his sleeve? I just been in my own lane, bro. Trying to stay out the way, that's all," Dreek said.

"I feel that I guess I need to get like you. I see you doing the domestic thing now. How that working out for you?"

"That old saying proving to be true. Hoes actually do turn out to be the best housewives. Shawty scarred just like me, bro and just need somebody who gon' love her past her body. I'm molding her into a woman, it's all good our way. I see you ain't been doing the domestic thing lately. What happened to Diamond?" Dreek wasn't the only one with the question.

Quay swallowed hard at the mention of his ex. "History, bro, she's ancient history."

***

Jasmine was in her small walk-in closet looking at herself in a full-length mirror trying to see how the miniskirt looked on her body. This was her fourth time changing trying to find the perfect assemble for her date with her new boo. His name was, Rinno. He was a very handsome Armenian man that she met in a Buckhead Star-bucks. He strolled in there one day and literally took her breath away. His 6"2 height, shiny shoulder-length hair, grayish-green eyes, and sophisticated swag, left her literally staring.

She quickly snapped out of the trance and focused back on the novel she was typing on her laptop. A few minutes later, he came and sat next to her on the couch she was on and surprised her with one of the most intellectual conversations she'd ever had with a man her age. Not only was he sexy, but he was also smart as well, and interested in her black ass. Six weeks later, and she was still feeling like it was all a dream.

The miniskirt was going to have to work because he was calling her phone to let her know he was outside. She answered, told him to give her a few minutes, and rushed to put the finishing touches on her appearance. She kissed Karma on the mouth and told the babysitter she'd be home late before leaving out.

They'd been out once a week since they'd met, so this would mark the sixth date for them. When she hopped in Rinno's BMW truck, he informed her that they had special reservations at the famous Bizzy's restaurant. She was excited about that because she'd always wanted to dine at Bizzy's.

They walked through the doors of the restaurant and checked in with the receptionist who told them to wait for the couple to finish up who was at their table.

"This place is so damn beautiful. Ronte shot a video in here before, so I've seen it before, but to actually see it with my own eyes is something totally different." She looked over at Rinno who wasn't nearly as impressed. "How many times have you been here? Matter-of-fact, the better question is— how many girls did you bring here already?"

He smiled that wonderful smile of his. A smile that could make a grown man seem as innocent as a newborn child. "Well, I've taken my mother out here about a dozen times, and just a few exes. Hopefully, this right here works out between us so neither one of us has to have another exe again."

He leaned over towards her and placed a loving kiss on her lips. She constantly underestimated her position, and presence, in his life. It was normal with women that he dealt with. They could've been the most arrogant, and prideful woman ever until he came into the picture, and they suddenly grew insecure, so he was used to reassuring them by now.

Neither of them saw Monster and Toe-Tag on their way out of the restaurant.

"Lil' G? Jassy! What the hell y'all got going on?" Monster stated while looking down at them surprisingly with Toe-Tag right beside him.

Jasmine looked up at Monster, then over at Rinno. "Lil' G, huh?"

"He told me you was fucking with one of the Dinero Girls, but I didn't know he hit that close to home, though. What the hell y'all in the waiting area for?" Monster asked.

"Waiting on our table," Rinno answered them, but he was looking at Jasmine who had suddenly grown quiet with a serious expression on her face.

Toe-Tag, and Monster, looked at each other with amused expressions. "This nigga always been the humble type. Boy, get yo' ass up! Yo' daddy would kill us if he knew we let you wait out here with all these regular folks."

Monster ushered them to their feet and demanded that the receptionist rescheduled them to dine at their usual table, that was free for another few hours anyway.

"A'ight, y'all enjoy y'all night and be safe. If y'all need something call me. Matter-of-fact, when y'all finish, I'll have a team out there waiting to escort y'all to y'all destination safely," Monster informed before walking off behind Toe-Tag.

They were escorted to their new table in the VIP section by one of the waiters. "Do you have a specific choice for the bottle of champagne. You won't be charged for anything, the big man put it on his tab."

"Ummm, Ace of Spade will be fine. Thanks," Rinno ordered once they were seated.

He clicked the button on the digital screen, and the curtain slid closed automatically covering the booth leaving them in their own little world.

As upset as Jasmine was she couldn't help but be distracted by the wonderfulness of the place. She'd never seen anything like it.

"Yeah, freaked me out when I first saw it too," he admitted trying to make her talk.

"I don't want to hear that shit, *Lil' G!*" she spat emphasizing his secret nickname.

"Come on, Jasmine. Don't be like that."

She shook her head disappointingly. She'd opened herself up to him since day one, and always stressed the importance of honesty to him. She didn't want any secrets between them, and he knew that, so the fact that Monster, and Toe-Tag, knew exactly who he was didn't sit right with her. Especially since he was just supposed to be the son of an architect.

"No, you don't be like that. We not supposed to keep shit away from each other, Rinno. You *know* how I feel about that. My last relationship wasn't shit. I'm trying to make this one better, but you not playing fair. I don't like that."

He leaned back in his seat with a heavy sigh. He looked dead at the woman he was falling for and moved the hair out of his face. "It's complicated, babe."

"I can handle it. Now please tell me who your father is for real this time."

CHAPTER 4

"God damnnn! Where this pussy ass nigga at, man!" Mooski barked from the backseat of his Escalade while looking out the window scanning the streets of Boulevard Avenue.

He was seeing red and could literally taste blood. He was high as a jet and going on his fifth day up without so much as a nap. Shit, his kill team was following in his footsteps, they weren't getting any sleep either. They were some livewires that were ready to blow.

Gutta bent a corner onto Daniel Street where Henny was known to kick it. He was the nigga that pointed them into Cable's direction when they asked him about his fighting dogs.

"That's his bitch right there! Let's snatch that hoe up! Pull over, G!" Mooski suggested while pointing at a chubby Latin woman who was standing in front of a corner store with a few other women.

Gutta kept driving down the street. "You tripping, bro'. She got her kids with her!"

"Fuck nigga, I don't care about that shit! I ain't gon' tell you no more to stop this muthafuckin' truck, Gutta!"

Gutta kept driving. Mooski was tripping, and he wasn't about to let him snatch that lady up who had nothing to do with the situation. Especially in front of her kids. He was probably the only person in Mooski's camp who wasn't scared of him. "You trippin', lil' bro! I can't do it."

Mooski pursed his lips with a mean mug on his face while nodding his head in understanding. He didn't say another word as they made their way back to the hood.

When they made it back to the hood, Gutta parked in front of Mooski's building. Mooski grabbed his gun and got out of the truck with his bird chest out leaving his shirt in the car.

"You need to get you some sleep, bro'. I'll make sure Babie makes it home safe," Gutta informed, after hopping out behind him.

Mooski looked at him awkwardly for a few seconds before bringing his right hand up with the gun still in it slapping Gutta upside the head with the chunk of metal.

"Aaahhh! What the fuck!" Gutta screamed in pain trying his best to defend himself from the oncoming assault Mooski was raining down on him.

"Shut the fuck up, nigga! Next time I tell you to do some shit, you do it nigga!" He had dropped the gun but was still raining punches down on him.

Trouble hopped out of the passenger's seat and rushed over to break the fight up. He was bigger and older than Mooski so it wasn't a problem for him to wrap him up in a bear hug and pull him up off Gutta. "Chill, bro!"

"T, if you don't let me go, I'm gon' knock the rest of your front teeth out!" Mooski promised with the seriousness of a supreme judge.

A midnight black AMG Benz pulled up, and the back window rolled down. "What the hell y'all niggas got going on?" Toe-Tag asked while scanning the scene.

Gutta was sitting up on the ground trying to stop the bleeding from his head, and Trouble still had Mooski wrapped up in a bear hug. It wasn't too hard to decipher the situation at hand.

He told Monster to put the truck in park before hopping out onto the concrete. "Let him go, Trouble."

Trouble did as he was told, and Mooski tried to pick his gun up but Toe-Tag's voice cut him short. "Leave it on the ground!"

"Ain't nothing going on, bruh. We good," he assured in an agitated tone.

Monster walked up toward them and put a hand on Toe-Tag's shoulder. "Let me handle this. You got too much shit going on to be dealing with this petty ass shit."

Toe-Tag shook his head in disagreement. "Nah, I'm already here, so I'm gon' handle it. Gutta, tell me what happened."

Gutta looked from Toe-Tag to Mooski, and back at Toe-Tag. "I was in the wrong about some shit, and Mooski was just on my ass about it. I tripped out and hit him in his shit, so he just did what any nigga would do. It's just like Monster said, though, some petty shit that don't deserve your time. We good," he lied with a straight face knowing how thin the line was that Mooski was on with Toe-Tag.

Toe-Tag squinted his eyes suspiciously before looking at Trouble who just shrugged his shoulders. "We good."

"You got some loyal niggas by your side. It'll be wise to start treating them right because ain't no telling how long that loyalty gon' last if they ain't receiving it in return," he warned Mooski before walking back to his truck and hopping in.

***

On the sixth floor of the Atlanta Medical Center, AK sat up in the hospital bed watching the local news nonchalantly. He wasn't processing any of the information because his mind wasn't there. He was reflecting hard on his strange life. Despite his newfound career, newfound purpose, and all the good deeds that he'd been carrying out since then, he still knew his past would come back and strike, but not that soon, and definitely not that hard.

The extremely unattractive Caucasian doctor that was assigned to him had just left his room a few hours ago. Since he was fully conscious during her visit, she decided to break the soul-crushing news to him.

"Mr. Kingston, I'm going to be completely honest with you. Upon your arrival, after I performed my first surgery on you, one of my nurses informed me of your profession and reputation. After that, I went into my office and pulled you up on YouTube. On one of your songs, the very first one I listened to, you stated that you're not scared of anything. I can understand why you said that, but it's definitely a false statement, Mr. Kingston. You can't say you're not scared of anything. Nobody can. There's always something you're going to be scared of, but you can be brave, and that's what you need to be right now. I'm sorry to tell you, but after a certain amount of healing, you'll be able to talk again, but your voice will be very low, and raspy. You'll never be able to rap again."

Her voice kept playing in his head. *"You'll never be able to rap again."* That piece of information wounded his soul to the core.

A single tear escaped from his eyes, but he refused to let the full river flow. He wasn't going to let the circumstance crush him.

Somehow, he would make it through the crisis. He still had his life, and he was 'definitely' blessed for it."

***

Toe-Tag stood up watching Lil' Tee sleep in his bed that was built like a Rocketship. The little nigga was starting to look more and more like him as he grew. He was two years old now and his obsession with his father made Toe-Tag kind of wish that he would've created a better future for the little nigga.

He kissed his son on the forehead before leaving his room. It was four o'clock in the morning, and he couldn't sleep to save his life. When he tried to sleep, he kept having nightmares about Silent's bitch ass. When he was up, his mind was always racing trying to either find a solution to an existing problem or trying to prevent an oncoming problem.

Even though he was doing considerably better than he was when he was out active in the field, he still had demons that still troubled him regularly. There was a steady light rain that fell outside, but that didn't stop him from getting dressed and leaving the apartment.

A few minutes later, he was standing in front of Lakisha's door.

"What's up, lil' nigga?" Mazi answered the door shirtless wiping the cold from his eyes.

"I'm gon' need you to climb out that pussy and get dressed."

Valencia was awakened from her sleep as well and summoned by the Don. Like Mazi, she didn't know why. All that was known is that Toe-Tag needed them, and that alone was enough for them.

They rode in silence as he gave Valencia directions to follow. A few short minutes after pulling out of the hood they were bending the curve in front of Sky Haven Elementary school.

"Stop here," Toe-Tag instructed suddenly. "Park right here and stay in the car. We'll be back in a few," he told Valencia before stepping out of the truck.

He started walking into the woods. "Where the hell we going, lil' bro?" Mazi asked from behind.

Toe-Tag didn't answer, he just cut the flashlight on from his waterproof iPhone and lead the way through the woods.

Right when Mazi was about to ask him the same question again, Toe-Tag stopped suddenly while pointing his flashlight towards the ground.

"What the fuck?" He looked down at the drop surprisingly. He would've never thought that the woods led to a cliff. "What's going on, Tee?"

Toe-Tag carefully lowered himself onto the ground and took a seat on the edge of the cliff causing his legs to dangle in the air. He didn't even care about the mud that was gushy from the rain. "Rampage down there."

"What!" Mazi asked looking at him like he'd lost his whole mind.

Toe-Tag took a deep breath and told the story about what happened to Rampage for the first time. Up until then, nobody but the people that were there that night knew exactly what happened to Rampage.

By the time he finished with the story, Mazi was sitting down on the ground next to him. He promised himself if he ever came across Vonte he would make him suffer for what he put his little brother through. "You did what you had to do, lil' bro. That's all. Don't let it beat you up."

Toe-Tag heard the words, but they did nothing to ease his soul.

Malik D. Rice

CHAPTER 5

Babie wouldn't get her finger back, but other than that, she was fine. She wasn't even too upset about losing her finger. It would take some getting used to, but shit happened. She was more worried about her man.

Mooski's behavior was getting worse. The demons in his body were definitely winning the war for his soul. One of the Mobsters that stayed at the hospital on her security detail informed her of the situation that happened between him and Gutta.

In a twisted way, she liked the fact that he was going so hard for her, but at the same time, she needed him to chill. He was already on a thin line with Toe-Tag and didn't want to lose him over his reckless behavior.

She looked over at him in the driver's seat bobbing his head to the music that was blasting from the speakers and came to the conclusion that he couldn't be changed, so she had to help him be the best psychopath he could be.

***

There was a big dice game in Paradise East. Get money niggas from all around gathered in the apartments for a chance to win big bucks and bragging rights. Amongst the crowd was Quay and his kill team.

He was watching one of his little homies do numbers on the dice when his phone vibrated from a notification. It was a message from Instagram, but he didn't know the person it came from. *You the reason AK got shot.*

He looked at the short message with wide eyes. Then he clicked on the profile, but there was no pictures to be seen.

He looked over at Turk who was watching the bet intensely and walked up to him. "Aye, look at this shit man."

Turk's expression went from agitation, to surprise as he read the message. "@*GotYoAss*?" he said the username out loud. "Who you think that is?"

"I don't know, man," Quay said shrugging his shoulders. "Gotta be Pooh Bear."

"Nahhh—I don't think that's his style right there. He too straight-forward. It got to be somebody he told."

Quay looked up at him with a worried expression. "What we gon' do?"

"Nooo, budddyyyy! I already told you what it was from the jump. I'm out of it, lil' nigga. This yo' problem and you need to man up and handle it."

The mystery person instructed Quay to meet them at the McDonald's downtown in Five Points. That worked well with Quay because it was a very public place, so he knew whoever it was didn't want to put a bullet in his skull.

"Ain't no pressure. That's exactly what I plan to do." He watched the rest of the dice game before hopping in his car to go handle business.

***

He walked into the building scanning the tables. He was looking for the only person that had on jewelry and found them quickly. "What the fuck?" he said aloud to no one particular.

DG Wopp sat there at the table looking up at him smugly. When he saw that Quay was stuck in place, he waved him over to the table. "Four's up."

"Fuck all that! What you doing here?" Quay stated totally disregarding the formal greeting.

Wopp smiled and leaned back in his seat. "I'm here because yo' ass rather play checkers than chess. At first, when Diamond took your money, you were in the right. You should've went to Toe-Tag then, and let him handle the problem accordingly, but you chose to take matters into your own hands to save your little pride. Long story short, you lost."

"How the hell did I lose?"

"Because you went through all that trouble to keep your little money, but you still won't be able to keep it because I already gave

Pooh Bear two-hundred and fifty gees to sit his ass down somewhere. And guess who gon' have to pay me?"

Quay's face balled up like an unborn baby. "Ain't nobody tell
you to do that sucker ass shit. I ain't paying shit!"

"You went through all this trouble to keep this away from Toe-
Tag for a reason. I guess he wouldn't be too happy about the situation. Especially if he had to come out of his pocket for your stupid-
ity."

***

After years of dining at Bizzy's, Freddy and Masio decided to
switch it up. They found another spot in Atlantic Station called Gold
Water. It was an upscale seafood joint that had some of the best
seafood chefs in the country at their disposal.

"That nigga gon' make me whack his bitch ass," Masio growled
aggressively. "I'll whack that nigga myself right about now. He got
me all the way fucked up."

He was upset about the new adjustments Kapo had just made in
the camp. He bumped Freddy up to the Pope and bumped Masio
down to the Capo over Atlanta. It wasn't really the fact that he had
been demoted, it was the fact that he would have to put some actual
work in now. He was used to sitting around, collecting a free
paycheck and Kapo was robbing him of that luxury.

"Before you might've been able to pull it off, but now— that
nigga's security detail is like the damn Secret Service. Them folks
be killing mosquitoes before they get a chance to bite the nigga."

Masio looked at his best friend with a straight face. "Fuck you,
Freddy!"

"I really don't know why you tripping, though. That Capo shit
ain't too complicated."

"Anything more complex than my old job is too complicated."

Freddy slurped up an oyster. "You gon' have to shake that lazy
shit. Plus, you did this to yourself anyway."

"What! How?"

"You the one that deprived the man of his retirement and gave him the chance to be the same exact nigga he is right now. That nigga's smart and knows exactly what he's doing. I told you to just let the nigga retire back then."

CHAPTER 6

Purp was one helluva nigga, any nigga who knew him, and what he was about, knew to keep him *far* away from their bitch. Unfortunately, Toe-Tag was paying him a visit for that exact reason.

They had an appointment set, and Purp chose to meet with him at the pool hall on Moreland Avenue since he had other business there anyway. The pool hall was having a good year in East Atlanta.

"Young nigga! What's good, how you been?" he asked Toe-Tag as they exchanged a brotherly embrace.

"Ain't shit old school, just trying to stay out the way, and stay alive."

"That's the best way to be. What was so important that made you crawl out that cave of yours?"

Toe-Tag paused for a second trying to decide how he wanted to approach the situation. The best way was head on. He'd never been the type to shy away from a situation. "One of my Mobsters found a conversation in his girl's text messages. Y'all been busy lately."

That earned a smile from Purp. "As you already know, I got too many bitches. You gon' have to be a little more specific."

Toe-Tag pulled his phone out and pulled up a picture of the woman on Instagram.

"Ohhhh, her! Yeahhhhh, she a lil' kinky bitch. What that got to do with me? I ain't in a relationship with the nigga, she is. He needs to take that up with her."

Toe-Tag showed him another picture of the same woman that his Mobster had sent him.

Purp knew it was her because of the tattoos on her body, but her face was unrecognizable. "Shiiitttt! The bitch looks dead!"

"Yeah, she is," Toe-Tag informed causally after putting his phone back in his pocket. "*Very* dead."

"I mean I'm not a fan of that particular behavior, but it's done. He handled his business, end of story."

Toe-Tag shook his head. "No, it's not the end yet. You see, my Mobster is an extremist, and if it was up to him you would've been laid in the picture next to her, but I convinced him otherwise." Purp just stared at him with wide eyes. "Yeah, I know—I saved your life old school, and that was hard work. Hard work that I need to get paid for," he informed with a devilish smirk, he couldn't help it.

***

"Hell nah! Don't do that. That's suicide for me," Dead Shot begged desperately.

Freddy being the spiteful individual he was, came up with the bright idea to demote Toe-Tag, and place Dead Shot in his spot.

"For you to be a seasoned killer, you, damn sure scary as hell," Freddy accused nastily.

"It don't got nothing to do with being scared. It's about being smart. How long you think I'm gon' last before I come up missing? I'm in the perfect position right now. I'm like a fly on the wall. That's what you need. That's what Vonte needs."

Freddy nodded his head slowly with his lips pursed together. "Get out of my limo."

***

Dead Shot pulled up into Sun Valley and was surprised at what he saw. There was a big crowd in the parking lot cheering on two men that were fighting in the middle of the crowd.

When he got out of his car and got a closer look at the action, he saw that it was Monster and Mazi in the middle of the crowd boxing. They had on UFC gloves and was athletically dressed for the occasion.

Monster was *very* quick for a man of his size, but he wasn't quicker than Mazi who wasn't that much smaller than him. Monster advanced on Mazi with a critical combination of punches that Mazi struggled to block. It was clear that he wasn't trying to get hit by any of the blows, but it was to no avail because Monster caught him with an uppercut that staggered him backward.

"Dlattttt!" The whole crowd spat in unison.

Dead Shot looked around in amazement at the crowd. They were one big strange family. They definitely shared a bond on a deeper level. They had a way of making outsiders feel like they were in a different world completely.

Mazi shook it off and recovered quickly. Monster advanced with another lethal combination, but Mazi had something for his ass this time. He blocked the first couple of punches with a few exotic block moves, then suddenly dropped down to the ground with amazing speed and popped back up even quicker with an uppercut of his own.

"Dlatttttt!"

About thirty seconds later, they ended the match as another two Mobsters stepped into the ring for some recreation.

"I ain't know yo' big ass could move like that there," Dead Shot said as he approached Monster who sat in a folding chair pouring water over his body getting a massage from, ZyAsia who acted as his coach.

"I'm getting old and slow. Too many drugs. Wassup, though?" Monster asked as they dapped one another up.

Dead Shot kneeled next to him, so he'd be able to hear him easily over the cheering crowd. "I'm just checking in, bro. Trying to see if it's something you need done or something. It's been a minute. You just backed up off a nigga out of nowhere."

"I just been going through shit, man. Trying to wrap my head around all this shit that's going on," Monster lied with a straight face.

Dead Shot nodded his head in understanding. "Just let me know whenever you need something done."

"Matter-of-fact, I do need you to handle something for me. AK is due to be transferred from Atlanta Medical to Grady. I need you, and your bodies to escort him. Then make sure he got security at Grady twenty-four/seven until he gets checked out."

"Say less, big bro. It's done," Dead Shot assured in a dedicated tone.

They shook hands, and Dead Shot walked off towards his car without so much as a backward glance, but he should've glanced back because he would've seen the unsettling look Monster was giving him.

CHAPTER 7

"I see now, you got a tendency of pulling up out here with these stupid ass requests. Nigga, ain't nobody tell you to do that sucker ass shit! You should've presented the problem to me, and I would've handled shit accordingly," Toe-Tag spat.

Wopp sat across from him once again with invisible steam rising from his bald head. "I wouldn't have to be out here if your Mobsters woulda stayed off my side of town with the fuck shit. I'm the one who got to deal with it, and that's what I did to prevent a war on my fucking turf! Don't make me take this over your head."

"Over *my* head? Who you gon' go to? Pablo? You know what, that's who you need to go to because I ain't paying yo' ass shit nigga! Now get up out my spot before I have these fellas remove you," Toe-Tag threatened sharply.

Monster and Mazi closed in on him for emphasis.

"Don't worry about it, your day gon' come. You just adding onto your list of enemies," Wopp promised.

Toe-Tag waved him off. "Wopp, get the fuck on before yo' ass don't make it back to the Southside."

He must've felt the threat because he left in a hurry, but Toe-Tag had no doubt he needed to add him on the long list of niggas that he needed to watch out for. More than enough people wanted him dead, and half of them stood on the same thing as him. That was the sad part.

"Damn, boy! Ain't no way Quay had all that shit going on the low," Monster stated surprisingly once Wopp was gone.

"Go find that nigga and tell him I said he needs to go out there and whack four crips. He can't take no kill team with him, or none of that shit. He started this mess by himself, so he gon' finish it that way. He not allowed back in the hood until it's done."

Monster nodded his head in understanding. He would've gone a little lighter on Quay, but Toe-Tag's word was law, so he left out to relay the message.

"Damn, boy," Mazi said after taking a seat next to his baby brother. "You got a lot on your plate."

Toe-Tag waved him off. "It is what it is. I'm just glad you out here to help a nigga carry some of this weight."

"You know I got you, lil' nigga. You doing a good job, though. I'm proud of you."

Someone rang the doorbell and Shanay answered it before either of them could. She looked through the peephole and opened the door. It was Babie. "Heyyy, lil' bitch!" Shanay greeted cheerfully.

"Move hoe! I need to talk to Tee," Babie spat while brushing past her not in the mood for their usual games.

Shanay looked back at her sideways before locking the door back and heading back into the kitchen to finish the meal she was preparing for the household.

"Can I talk to you?" Babie asked Toe-Tag as she stood over him and Mazi with her undamaged hand on her small hip.

"Yeah, I guess. Take a seat," Toe-Tag answered while motioning on the other side of the wraparound sofa.

"*Alone*," she emphasized eyeing Mazi.

Mazi turned his nose up at the little brat. "Who the hell you think you is, coming in here making demands?"

"Princess Babie, nigga!" she spat matching his tone.

"Y'all chill! Let me chop it up with her real quick, bro. You need to go spend some time with your nephew anyway," Toe-Tag said.

Mazi got up reluctantly, and went to the backroom, but not before ice grilling Babie's little sassy ass.

"Babie, you can't be mean to every damn body. Especially not Mazi. You might have to come to him for a favor one day."

She took a seat in Mazi's old spot. "I really been nice lately compared to how I used to be. I guess I'm just frustrated right now, that's all. Look at this shit, bro! I'm a muthafuckin' handicap now!"

Seeing Rampage's little sister with a bandage over her hand infuriated him to the highest power. He promised his friend to always take good care of his sister, so it didn't sit right with him. "You not handicapped, girl. You need to be thankful because it could've been worse. Matter-of-fact, tell Mooski when they find the nigga that sent him down there, not to kill him. I'm gon' end him my damn self!"

Babie nodded her head understandingly. "That's really why I came over here to talk to you."

"Mooski?" he asked.

"Yeah." He stared at her waiting on her to continue. "What happened between y'all? Shit ain't been the same between y'all since we swapped hoods."

He shook his head in disagreement. "No, shit ain't been the same between us since I stopped playing with my nose. Which yo' lil' ass need to do as well."

"Well, you the one that introduced him to the shit, Tee! That nigga looked up to you like Superman. He used to be at peace when you kept him close around. Now, he just—"

"Just what?"

She ran her good hand through her weave. "The boy needs guidance, Tee. Just think about it. I'm about to go get some rest, I'm tired."

"Aye!" He stopped her on her way out the door.

"Yeah."

"I'm serious about what I said about playing with yo' nose. Leave that shit alone, Babie."

***

Black was exiting the building of the church that he and his family had just joined. He came down the church steps holding Ciara's hand with one of his, and their son's hand with the other. His Sunday was peaceful until he looked up and saw the unsettled look on Quay's face. He stood outside of his Audi leaning on the passenger's door looking up at them blankly.

"What's good, fam? You alright?" asked Black once he made it to his friend.

Quay nodded his head. "I just need to talk to you real quick."

Black told Ciara to take Vernon to his car in the parking lot and wait for him. "Talk to me, bro. You look like shit."

"You ain't gon' believe this shit here."

"Hit me with it," Black encouraged.

Quay told him everything that happened since the situation with Diamond and everything he had to do now.

"Damn. Why you ain't just go to Toe-Tag after she ran off with your shit man?"

"I don't know, man. I guess I ain't want it to look like I went out bad." Quay always kept it real with Black.

Black shook his head. "Pride is a man's biggest downfall. Look at you now, you going out worse. Look, you been doing this shit for a minute, and you definitely not new to this shit no more That's the life you want, you got it, bro. Handle that business, and put this shit behind you. All you can do is try to do better in the future. I got to go, my family's waiting on me. I love you, lil' nigga."

Quay watched his best friend walk away. In a way, he wanted to be mad at him, but how could you be mad at someone who just wants the best for you, and never told you anything wrong?

It was right then he noticed his mistake. He shouldn't have come to Black. Black wasn't in the game anymore, and it wasn't fair for him to try and drag him back into the same world he worked so hard to get out of. He made a vow to distance himself from Black, it was for the best.

CHAPTER 8

Toe-Tag walked into AK's new hospital room. He was impressed by the security that was posted outside the door. AK was a vital piece of the camp and needed to be protected just as much as he did. He was just as important. Their relationship was kind of weird at first considering the content of their past, but as two head honchos over the camp, they put the past behind them and stuck together to carry the weight of the camp. AK was the voice, and Toe-Tag was the enforcement.

AK was laid up in the bed with his dreads tied up looking at an old episode of *Maury* on the flat-screen TV that hung from the wall. When the door opened, his eyes left the TV and settled on Toe-Tag.

"My brother, wassup? I just dropped in to check on you personally. The doctor told me that you can talk but it's a big and painful effort. So, just let me do the talking. Anything you got to say, you can just write it down on that pad they gave you that you ain't been using. I found out who was behind your shooting."

As expected, AK's eyes grew larger, and he sat up a little more. He started to part his chapped lips to talk but was stopped short by Toe-Tag's sharp voice. "*I said*—don't talk nigga!"

Toe-Tag told him all about the events that led up to his incident, and all the events that are yet to come in the nearby future. When he was finished, he just looked down at AK who looked up at him through squinted eyes.

AK grabbed the notepad on the nightstand next to his bed for the first time since it had been placed there by the nurse.

Toe-Tag stood on the fourth floor of the hospital reflecting on AK's words he read on the notebook paper.

I don't know how you gon' do it, but you need to make this shit right!

The elevator door opened, and Ronte stepped off with his entourage.

Ronte hated Toe-Tag for taking Vonte away from him, and Toe-Tag hated Ronte for the simple fact that he looked exactly like Vonte. This was their first time face-to-face, and the tension in the air was thick. Neither said anything to the other. Toe-Tag just stepped onto the elevator and locked eyes with Ronte as the doors closed.

"What the fuck he doing here?" Mazi asked confused.

"AK fuck with the nigga for some reason. Guess he going to check up on him."

***

It amazed Quay how the thought of killing someone else didn't faze him, but the thought of him getting killed didn't sit right with him. He just wasn't ready to face the Grim Reaper just yet, which is why he went so hard to make sure that he lived on as long as humanly possible.

Toe-Tag said he couldn't come back to the hood unless he whacked four crips. Personally, he thought Toe-Tag was overreacting but who was he to question the Don's authority. He was in the wrong, and it was on him to face the consequences.

"Damnnn," he whispered to himself as he saw a super thick, half-naked stripper walking to her car in the parking lot of the duplex housing he was in. "I know them plastic surgeons getting crazy money these days."

He adjusted himself in the driver's seat of his car. He was comfortable in a pair of cutoff True Religion jeans, a Ralph Lauren tank top, and Adidas slippers, but he was still getting tired of sitting there. He'd been in the car staking out the same spot going on five hours.

"I should just go in there and handle business right now. Nah, got to play it smart," he reasoned to himself before rolling up another blunt of weed and starting his music playlist over. This was about to be a long night.

Meanwhile, inside her duplex, Diamond stood at her window with a pair of binoculars up to her eyes peeping through her blinds. Her heart was racing and she couldn't stop tapping her foot, normal behavior when she was nervous.

She pulled her phone out of her pants pocket and made a call. "Bear, I don't know what the hell you doing or why you not answering your phone. But you need to hurry up and call me back man! Hurry up, it's serious!" She tossed her phone onto the couch and put the binoculars back up to her eyes. "I should go out there and handle business right now by myself."

***

Henny had just got back in town from a trip to Washington DC. There was a big dog fight up there, and he just had to go win some big bucks. He took one of his most prized dogs and ended up winning $43,000 on two fights. Not bad for a few days of work. He pulled up to his one-story house right off Boulevard Avenue. He ushered the dog from the back of the Suburban into the backyard with her two brothers. He had a small pack, but they were *very* lethal.

He walked toward the house with a sigh. He told his little brother not to have any parties at the house while he was gone, but that command obviously went in one ear and out the other. He entered through the back door into the kitchen. As he stood there at the back door, he could see the whole kitchen and living room. They were having a party alright.

His little brother, E.J. was on the couch next to Mooski getting lap dances from two half-naked girls he'd never seen before. Shit, he hadn't seen anyone in the house before except for Mooski, and Gutta. The other five niggas, and eight females were very new faces.

"Bro!" E.J. waved him into the living room where he sat in a chair next to Mooski.

"Didn't I tell you no parties? It's two o'clock in the morning man! I'm trying to get some sleep."

Mooski shook his head. "Nah, this right here is a celebration, my guy. I struck big when you put me on that redneck Cable."

"That's good, but we could've celebrated another time. Right now I got a headache, and I'm tired from the long drive. I just came from Washington."

"Damn, Washington? I bet you won some good money up there. I just really wanted to thank you for putting me onto your plug, bro.

Go back to your room and look on your bed I got a lil' present for you just to show my appreciation."

Henny sighed and walked down the hall into his bedroom. He tossed his book bag on the floor and flipped on the light switch. "Ohhhh!" He took two rapid steps back and tripped on the second one falling back onto his ass on the hardwood floor.

His breathing had picked up, and his brain was working overtime trying to make sense of the fact that Cable's very dead body was laying on his bed in a large plastic bag with the air vacuumed out of it.

He struggled back onto his feet and rushed into the living room just to receive another shock. "Wait! Wait! What the hell you got going on, Mooski? What's going on, bro? Talk to me!"

Two Mobsters held E.J. down on his knees while Gutta held one of his hands on the table.

Mooski brought him up to speed on everything that happened down in Glenville that day.

"Wait! It wasn't anything funny going on! That was Cable's brother! He's always in the cut to make sure nobody tries anything funny with them. Just as a safety precaution."

"He shot first."

"You said your girl pointed at him. He probably got spooked and shot."

Mooski nodded his head in understanding. "Whether it was a misunderstanding, or not. I still had to watch my girl lose a finger, so it's only right that you watch your brother lose four."

E.J. started screaming before Gutta brought the machete down onto his left hand. Every finger except for his thumb was completely severed. He started screaming louder as he watched the blood shoot out from his hand.

"Noooooo!" Henny rushed over to help his brother, but one of the Dinero Girls stuck her foot out and tripped him causing him to crash to the ground.

Mooski walked up to him slowly with his Glock 18 out and put it to the back of his head. "That would've been you, but I got orders not to touch you. So, I got your brother instead."

CHAPTER 9

Quavo was in his bedroom chilling with his right-hand-man, Ricardo. They were thick as thieves. The only reason they didn't spend as much time together as they used to was because Monster had placed them in two different camps. Quavo ended up with Dreek, and Ricardo ended up with Mooski.

Unlike Dreek, who took it easy on the younger Mobsters, Mooski made *everyone* in his camp put in work. His logic was that if they wanted to be in the game, they had to put in the proper work. There were no free rides.

"Man, I'm telling you I was right there holding the nigga down when Gutta chopped that nigga fingers off! Blood everywhere, bro! I was like what the fuck! That shit was crazy!"

Quavo felt like less of a Mobster because he couldn't hit Ricardo back with an interesting story of his own. "Mooski be letting y'all have all the fun, man. Dreek might let a nigga do something here and there, but for the most part, we just be in the hood slow motion."

"You lucky. That murder life ain't no hoe, bro. Imagine seeing what you saw that night every other day. Shit, I be having to get up close and personal with the bodies when we clean 'em up sometimes. Shit's crazy."

"Yeah, he right. That murder life ain't no hoe, and you need to be grateful you ain't got to go through the same shit as yo' friend here," Mazi stated as he snuck up on them. "Let me chop it up with this lil' nigga real quick," he told Ricardo.

Ricardo went into the living room and Mazi took a seat on the floor with Quavo. "You got a good friend right there. Instead of glorifying the shit, he's giving it to you raw."

"Yeah, I know," Quavo said.

Mazi could see that the young nigga was uncomfortable, so he draped an arm around his small shoulder. "I'm not here to give you no lecture, or nothing. I know your mind's made up, and you chose to be a Mobster, and that's alright. Shit happens. Yo' mamma ain't told me yet, but I can tell the fact that you're in the streets is fucking with her, so I got an idea. If you gon' be a Mobster, I might as well make sure you're being the best you can be."

"What you saying?" Quavo asked looking up at his new idol.

"I'm gon' take you up under my wing and put you in my camp."

"What about Dreek?"

"That's my lil' nigga, let me handle him."

Neither one of them saw Lakisha standing in the hall listening in on their conversation.

***

"Speak English, man! I told you about using all them big ass words I don't know yet!" Toe-Tag spat irritably.

He was in his condo at the dining room table having a meeting with a potential movie director.

"Baeeee, stop being mean!" Shanay advised.

The director was a heavyset dark man. "It's alright, he did warn me. My apologies, I'll cut the extreme vocabulary because I want you to understand me, and there's no business without understanding. As I was saying, I have formed and managed a production company in the past, but got an offer from a bigger company to buy me out, and I accepted. That's why I'm now independent, but under the right terms, I'll defiantly collide with you for the upcoming projects."

Toe-Tag leaned back in his chair. "What terms?"

"Ten percent of the company."

Toe-Tag's phone vibrated, he looked at the text from Mooski and could hear the excitement in his voice just from reading the text.

//: Got ya boy with me. On the way to the warehouse now. You still want to handle it yourself?

"I'll get back with you on that one." He got up and started rolling the sleeves up on his button-down Dior shirt.

"Where you going?" Shanay asked.

"Got some other business that needs to be handled real quick. Go ahead and start cooking, I'll be home for dinner."

***

This was Quay's second day on the prowl. The night before, he caught two crips slipping, and did them the worst way. He could've easily slayed two more and had the whole ordeal over with, but those last two slots belonged to Diamond, and Pooh Bear, since they were the cause of all his current problems. He still had on the same attire as the day before, and the same AK-74 on his lap that he slayed his last two victims with. He was back in Diamond's parking lot across the street from her new townhouse eating a Slim Jim waiting for her to come out.

"Bitch, you ain't never stayed in the house this much. Got yo' ass shook! You know wassup!" He said to himself. He was so busy texting his girlfriend that he almost missed her walking to her car. "Got yo' ass now!"

He wanted so bad to hop out and walk up on her now, but the area they were in wouldn't make that a very smart idea. He'd end up in a shootout with the police, and didn't plan on that, so he waited for her to pull out and followed her outside the subdivision.

The townhouses were in a suburban area of Clayton county. He followed her all the way to Old National Boulevard and prepared to make his move on her before she got to her destination. Judging from the route she was taking he knew she was on the way to her mother's house.

She turned onto the backstreets and he unbuckled his seat belt while getting in his kill zone. He couldn't even wait he was itching for the kill. Once she stopped at the first stop sign, he hopped out the car with his gun up and ready.

She had two cars ahead of her, and they all were waiting for a lady to finish pushing this old man in a wheelchair across the street. He saw the perfect opportunity and took it. Once he got to the car, he opened fire on the blue Lexus that Diamond drove. He could hear her screaming, and it only geeked him up more. As he expected, she tried to pull off, but he was on her ass. He was about to pick his speed up but felt a stinging sensation in his left leg, he'd been shot.

He looked behind him as he stumbled to the ground and saw a whole motorcade of motorbikes approaching. He was so zoned out on Diamond that he must've missed them. He cursed himself inwardly as he lifted his gun and opened fire at the motorcade as he fell onto the ground.

"Aaahhhh!" He caught another bullet to the shoulder of the arm that he held the gun in causing it to *clang* onto the ground. Seconds later, he was surrounded by dirt bikes and blue bandanas.

"Damn, shawty!" he spat before resting his head on the concrete looking up at the blue sky.

"You, *damn* right!" Pooh Bear retorted after pulling his bandana from over his face. "Get this nigga back to the spot!" he commanded before burning rubber on the four-wheeler popping a wheelie. "Clattt!"

"I could've got shot nigga!" Diamond spat once Pooh Bear walked into their mother's house.

"I wasn't gon' let you get shot girl, shut up."

Their mother walked into the living room eating from a box of chocolates. "Where he at? Y'all got the nigga that kidnapped my baby? I want to see him bleed, Pooh Bear! You hear me?"

Pooh Bear nodded. "Yeah, ma, I got you. I'm gon' get it all on video for you."

"I want to see that nigga bleed, too!" Lil' Man barked as we walked into the room gripping the pearl 380. that Pooh Bear gave him from Christmas. "I want to kill him myself!"

CHAPTER 10

After Rampage's death, Jasmine basically turned into a loner. She barely had to leave her apartment. She took care of Karma and wrote her books when she was sleep. She really needed that solitary time to learn and bond with herself. She'd done so much growing in the past eight months, and she was proud of the woman that she was growing into.

Besides Karma and Rinno she didn't have anyone else to associate with. She was at home watching Karma play by herself and thought about the days she used to play with Lil' Tee in the hood. The thought of taking a trip to the hood and paying her old friend, Shanay a visit crossed her mind, but she decided against it. She promised herself she wouldn't step foot back into the hood for anyone and planned on keeping that promise, so she invited Shanay over to her apartment.

They sat on the soft carpeted floor in Karma's room and watched the kids play with each other.

"You got a nice spot, girl. I'm glad you're independent and doing good for yourself. I'm proud of you, bitch," Shanay informed honestly.

"Thank you, girl. Sorry I haven't been in touch, just been trying to get right with myself."

Shanay waved her off dismissively. "Girl, you ain't got to do all that. I know what's going on. Plus, I've been going through my own internal tribulations being a mob wife and all. You know the motions."

"You know it! But you're training Tevin right, though. It's looking like he might actually last on his throne."

Shanay breathed a heavy breath. "I pray he do. He's smarter than what he gives himself credit for. I know he got what it takes. He just got to sit his ass down. I think he got his hands dirty last night."

"That nigga's like a vampire girl. He got to get some blood every once in a while. Guess what?"

"What?"

"I been fucking with this young rich nigga. He acted like he was a square at first, but come to find out, his daddy's a whole mob boss."

"Bitch, ain't no wayyy! You done hit the damn jackpot! You better not fuck this up!"

Jasmine had a strong sense for people and could see the genuine happiness Shanay was expressing for her. Seeing how happy she was for her made Jasmine realize how much of a real friend Shanay was. She promised right then and there to keep Shanay close. Everyone needed someone to share their happiness with.

"I'm thinking about introducing him to my mother."

"Give it some time, baby girl. The relationship is still new. You don't want to move too fast and fuck shit up."

Jasmine gave her a hug. "I love you, girl!"

"I love you, too, Jassy," Shanay admitted hugging her back.

They took comfort in each other. They both needed each other at the moment. Their reunion couldn't have come at a better time.

***

Wopp sat in the bleachers with his seven-year-old daughter on his lap watching his oldest son on the basketball court do his thing. Times like this made it all worth it. He loved his kids, and at times wished that he was just a regular father that could be there for them a little more, but he'd already sold his soul to Dilluminati and that couldn't be taken back. Freddy made sure of that. He put his problems to the side and focused back on the game, and how peaceful he felt with his daughter on his lap clapping for her big brother. He had his phone on airplane mode because he didn't want to be disrupted from his family time, and his Don's knew this, which is why his top Don, Mario came strolling into the high school gym with his full kill team behind him.

He knew right then something was very wrong because Mario wouldn't dare pull a stunt like this for anything less than a critical emergency, so he stood up, placed his daughter on her feet, and walked down the bleachers to meet with Mario who stood on the sidelines staring at him knowingly.

"Sorry to interrupt you, big bro', but shit done got hectic just that quick," Mario informed as he approached.

"What now?"

Mario wanted to tell him but figured he'd be better off pulling his phone out and showing him instead.

Wopp looked at the video on Mario's phone with wide eyes, and an open mouth. The video started with a masked man talking shit about Dilluminati who then turned the camera onto Quay who was tied to the top of a car like a mattress. He was naked and bleeding all over like he'd been cut with a razor countless times. The masked man then passed the camera off to someone else who recorded him doing donuts in an empty lot with Quay still on top.

"What the fuck, Mario?"

"Don't *what the fuck* me! I'm just as confused as you. What you want me to do because that's one of Toe-Tag's Mafioso's. The Southside about to be on fire after this one right here."

Wopp couldn't even be mad at Mario for the fear he saw in his eyes. Shit, he was scared his damn self. This wasn't something that could be talked out. Atlanta had another major war on its hands.

***

Toe-Tag stood on top of the playground set with Mazi beside him, holding a meeting with his Mafioso's and their kill-teams. The video with Quay went viral and pained him deeply. He felt responsible for Quay's fate and wouldn't stop until Pooh Bear had forty-four bullets in his body.

"We sliding on them niggas by the day! Them niggas think they just did some shit? We gon' show them fuck niggas! We 'bout to make Rampage proud with this body count right here!" His blood was boiling and he was seeing red.

He wasn't worried about the series he was in the midst of producing, he wasn't worried about jail, and he damn sure wasn't worried about death. He just wanted revenge, and to hopefully get Quay back with some breath still in his body.

He looked up and saw Turk approaching with a handful of his soldiers. He felt at ease knowing that they had the backup of PDE on their side. He jogged down the slide to meet with them on the ground.

"What's good, bro?" he asked as they shook hands.

Turk shook his head as he stared Toe-Tag in the eyes intensely. "Check this out, everybody knows how much I fuck with that young nigga Quay. I feel like shit for not helping him when he came to me, but you—" He pointed a stern finger in Toe-Tag's face. "You was supposed to take better care of him, shawty. You ain't have to be that hard on him, so this—all this is on you! It's on y'all! PDE ain't taking no parts in this shit."

Toe-Tag's face crumbled instantly. "Fuck you mean y'all not taking no parts? You come over here claiming how much you fuck with Quay then gon' tell me you ain't riding! You gon' leave a nigga you fuck with in the water like that?"

Turk laughed in Toe-Tag's face. "You a damn fool if you think Quay's still alive. You killed him when you sent him on that suicide mission."

Toe-Tag watched him walk away with clenched teeth. He was beyond angry and hoped Turk was wrong about Quay.

CHAPTER 11

Kapo was at his new Shoreside mansion in San Fransisco that 2-Tall talked him into buying on one eventful drunk night. He'd bought the house three months ago, yet, this was his first time actually stepping foot inside the place. He stood in the huge kitchen contemplating if he wanted to resell the place. He really had no use for the place, renting might be a good idea. That way he'd have more legal income flowing. The worst thing about money and power is the decisions that come with them. Every adult make decisions but a rich adult makes many more.

He was enjoying the peaceful time alone until Glock walked into the kitchen holding one of his phones. "Phone call, boss."

"Who?"

"2-Tall," he answered before handing Kapo the phone and leaving back out the room.

"Talk to me."

"Where are you?" 2-Tall asked sternly.

The usual friendly tone he used with Kapo was gone, and it alerted him. Something was wrong. "I'm in San Fransisco. Why what's up?"

"You need to get back to Georgia asap!"

Before Kapo could ask what happened, 2-Tall, hung up and sent him the video of Quay. Kapo didn't have any words after watching the video. He just let out a low whistle while shaking his head.

***

Masio pulled up into Sun Valley apartments for the first time in years. Shit, it'd been a while since he'd been in East Atlanta period. Being back in the field like this felt kind of weird. He'd been on his high horse for so long. The sun was descending, so he parked his money green E-class Benz up under a streetlight in the heart of the complex while his security parked their Escalade parallel to him.

He stepped outside the car and looked around. The apartments had come a long way since he'd last stepped foot in them before they got remodeled.

"What you need, old school?" A young Mobster asked as he approached Masio with two more Mobsters behind him."

"*Old school*? You know who I am? You better put some respect on my name. It's Capo Masio to you, lil' nigga. Now take me to Toe-Tag," he barked at the tattooed delinquent.

The Mobsters ended up showing Masio, and his security, the way to Toe-Tag's condo. He didn't even have to walk inside because Toe-Tag was in front of his building amidst a half-dozen Escalades. They were suiting up for a long night. Masio was literally right on time.

"I was expecting one of the higher-ups to come down here, but I definitely wasn't expecting you," Toe-Tag admitted as he closed-in on Masio and shook hands with him. It was their first time meeting face to face.

"Yeah, unfortunately, Kapo saw fit to demote me to Capo, so I got to deal with live wires like you."

"I'm sorry to hear the bad news, but unfortunately you wasted your time because it's nothing for us to talk about."

Masio grew a smirk as he stood there and eyed the young boss. "Listen, I've been where you are right now, youngin. You feel like you don't have another choice, but you do. That's just your pride talking, right now. Let us handle this shit the right way."

"Masio, I ain't got nothing against you and I'm sorry you had to be the one to come down here and talk some *sense* into my head, but I wouldn't give a fuck what you stood right here and said. We sliding on them niggas regardless." The determination in Toe-Tag's eyes was fierce and unmistakable.

Masio saw it too. "You do know you might face consequences after this war is over, right?"

"Maybe," he admitted as he shrugged his shoulders nonchalantly. "I'll just have to deal with that once the smoke clears."

***

The very next morning, a few hours before the sun was due to rise Monster reunited with his pack. Toe-Tag relayed a coded message to him while he was in Miami, and he took the next flight back to ATL. He was so furious when he saw the video of Quay. He was instructed to meet them in front of Sky Haven Elementary school.

He drove his Range Rover around the corner and called Toe-Tag. "Where y'all at?"

"You don't see Dreek in front of the school by the woods?"

Monster scanned the street. "Yeah, I see him now. You got this black ass nigga out here like a roach in the night."

He parked his car down the street and walked back to where he saw Dreek who escorted him to their destination.

Monster had been in East Atlanta all his life and had never known about this patch of woods. He didn't roam on this side of Flat Shoals. He wondered how Toe-Tag found this spot, but those suspicions would have to be put on hold because there were obviously more important matters to handle at the moment.

There were four men were lying face down on the ground naked tied up with duct tape while a good amount of Mobsters surrounded them with flashlights and guns in their hands. It's like they were waiting for something.

"Took you long enough. We been waiting on you. Bad enough you missed the kidnappings, I couldn't let you miss this," Toe-Tag stated as Monster approached.

Monster kneeled to get a closer look at the hostages. "One of these niggas know what happened to Quay?"

"I don't know, let's find out," Toe-Tag said before ordering a few of the Mobsters to roll the men over onto their back's where they could see what was going on.

Toe-Tag helped the first nigga onto his feet. He couldn't walk because of the duct tape wrapped around his legs, and ankles, so he hopped towards the cliff as Toe-Tag guided him. Once Toe-Tag stopped, and one of the Mobsters shined their flashlights on what was supposed to be the ground, his eyes got huge and he started mumbling something behind the duct tape that was secured over his mouth.

Toe-Tag ripped the duct tape off his mouth. "What was that? You know something about Quay?"

"Hell nah, man! I don't know shit. I ain't have nothing to dooooohhhh—" he was saying before being pushing by Toe-Tag and falling at least thirty feet to the ground.

Unless he fell on his neck, he wasn't dead but he was sure to have some broken bones, and he would lay right there until he either starved to death or got bit by a poisonous spider or something. It didn't make Toe-Tag any different, as long he suffered a slow death.

Toe-Tag turned around, walked back toward the other three men, and instructed one of the Mobsters to remove the duct tape from the next man's mouth. "I hope you know something."

***

Meanwhile, on the Southside Mooski and his kill team were hard at work. They'd completed the first phase of their mission by shooting up just about every known chill spot for the crips on the Southside. It wasn't easy and they'd barely made it out of a few spots, but it was done. Now, it was time for them to head back to the east side.

"Shittt!" Mooski barked holding his stomach while grimacing intensely.

"What the hell wrong with you?" asked Gutta looking over at him.

"Man, I'm hungry as fuck. We got to go grab something to eat."

"We'll be back on the Eastside in about thirty minutes," Trouble informed from behind the wheel.

Mooski shook his head rapidly. "Fuck that, we can just hit one of these drive-thrus up real quick."

"That's a bad call, Mooski. We sitting ducks out here," Gutta tried to rationalize with his seemingly brainless friend.

"Just chill, man. You see this shit?" Mooski held up his new Keltec PLR16 with a drum attached that held 223 AR bullets. "I wish a nigga would!"

Mooski decided on a Mcdonald's store right outside of College Park. He told the rest of the Mobsters in the truck behind them to drive ahead to the hood. It was just him, Gutta, and Trouble in their truck. He ordered a Southern-style chicken sandwich with large fries and a medium Sprite. The employee told them to park in the parking lot, and their order would be delivered to them shortly.

"I got to take a piss," Trouble informed uneasily while looking back at them through the rearview mirror.

"What the fuck wrong with y'all niggas? Y'all acting like this a regular night out in the town. We just did seven drive-bys in the same night. Ain't no way we still on the damn Southside, man," Gutta stated irritably.

"Just like you said, we just put in all that work. We deserve a break. We gon' make it back to the hood, you acting like folks on our ass or something," Mooski countered. "Go take a piss by that tree, Trouble. Hurry yo' ass up."

As Trouble walked toward the tree in the shadows, Gutta took a deep breath and sunk down low in his seat. He was tired of Mooski's poor decisions. After this was all over, he was going to send a request to Toe-Tag to switch his Mafioso. He loved Mooski like a brother but the guy sitting next him wasn't Mooski anymore.

"Oh, shittt!" Mooski spat suddenly.

Gutta sat up rapidly. "What?"

"Look!" Mooski pointed at Trouble who was still pissing on the tree with a light shining on him. That light came from a police cruiser.

The policeman and his partner got out of the car and started walking toward Trouble who was fumbling to put his dick back into his pants.

"Once they see that DG tattoo on his face, they gon' ask him for I.D, and shit gon' get ugly after that," Mooski predicted.

All three of them had warrants out for their arrest from a home invasion they pulled a couple of months ago. There were hidden cameras, and it was one of those nights that they didn't wear masks.

"Damn, I told y'all niggas!" Gutta spat intensely.

"Shut up! The only reason they stopped him is because he was pissing on the tree. Damn, he about to run!"

Just like Mooski predicted, Trouble ran. He ran away from the truck and took them out of harm's way. As expected, both officers chased him. One on foot, the other in the cruiser. Mooski and Gutta took a deep breath once they were out of sight. "You think he gon' get caught?" asked Gutta.

Mooski nodded his answer. "Definitely, that nigga got the lungs of an old lady. Might as well text the lawyer now. Get in the driver's seat, I'm ready to go."

"What about your food?" Gutta asked while climbing to the front of the truck.

"Lost my appetite."

CHAPTER 12

2-Tall was only twenty-nine years old, and still trying to get a grip on life and actually understand it all. He'd literally transformed worlds within a matter of years. He went from a Porsche and a chain to a private jet and a small string of jewelry stores. He played it cool on the outside because that's what he did, but on the inside, he felt a little uncertain. It all seemed so good to be true, like a dream. It was very frustrating because he was lifting a terrible amount of responsibility on his shoulders.

Those were insecurities he felt he couldn't really share with anyone. He couldn't go to Malina with his problems because she too expected him to have it all figured out. He was starting to come to the realization that he would probably live the rest of his life as a prisoner in his own mind.

He flew back to New York City to stop by at the DG Records studio with his little homie, Flipp who was weeks short from dropping his debut album. He cut his eyes at his baby's mother, Demi, and caught her staring at him.

"You got a whole boyfriend. It's not polite to stare at another man like that."

"Fuck you, Terrio! You know how I feel about you. You the one that left me and sold your heart to a cartel princess."

He slapped his head and leaned back in the adjustable chair. "Ever since I've been with you, I've been telling and showing you that *everything* I do is for us. You better open your mind up because I'm elevating by the day. You focused on the wrong shit, shorty."

She started rambling about something but 2-Tall had cut her off because Malina was calling his phone, and he had to answer because she knew he was with Demi. He got up and stepped out of the studio into the hallway.

"My beautiful, Goddess," he answered brightly.

"Humph, I'm not trying to hear that smooth talk bullshit. I'm still mad at you."

"I don't know why. It's not like I'm creeping. You know I'm not stupid enough to cheat on you man."

She signed heavily. "Whatever, guess who surprise visited me this afternoon?" She didn't even give him a chance to reply. "My uncle!"

"I thought George was in Italy."

"His Italy is really Egypt. You'll never know where he really is, but that's not important. What's important is why he popped up on me."

"How about you hurry up and tell me."

"He wants to meet with you face to face," she informed matter-of-factly. She was overwhelmed so she could only imagine how he felt.

2-Tall paused for a second but recovered quickly. "Damn, the old man finally came around. That's wassup, it's a date." He wrapped the conversation up with her and stuck the phone in his pocket.

He had a sudden headache, his mind was rambling for a good reason. Why George would want to meet with him personally? He didn't even bother to go back in the studio. He continued down the hallway toward the elevators with his security shadowing him carefully.

*****

AK sat up in the hospital bed looking at the embarrassing video of Quay. It was up to over 6 million views in a matter of days. It was a big blow to the gut for Dilluminati. He'd been trying to call Toe-Tag but wasn't receiving any responses, and he understood completely. Toe-Tag was responsible for Quay, so that wasn't a good look on him.

AK dropped his phone on the bed and placed both hands firmly on the bed as he made a minor effort to stand. He stood successfully, then came the steps. It was his first time walking since he'd been shot a few weeks ago. His neck was aching from the heavy breathing, and dizziness was falling upon him, so he returned to the bed unenthusiastically.

Maybe it was the high dose of Percocet they were shooting inside his bloodstream, but at first, he was optimistic about the unfortunate situation, now he just didn't know. From everything that was going on and all those long and hard hospital days piling up, he felt useless. The realization settled in that his gift was snatched from him, and he could feel the anger rising from within. That inner demon resurfacing.

The door opened and Pretty walked in looking like the ratchet princess she was. She was considered basic to him these days, but that was only on the outside. On the inside, she was one of the most beautiful people he'd ever had the chance to meet.

"Aww, look at you sitting up looking all strong and whatnot," she cheered as she dropped her bags on the floor and took a seat on the bed next to him.

"Turn that shit off," he spat sharply, but his voice was now just over a whisper and hurt like hell when he did talk. He would sound like Darth Vader's son for the remainder of his life. He couldn't stand the beautiful sound of his old voice.

Pretty fumbled with her phone to turn the music off. "I'm sorry, baby. I understand why you're upset, but I'm just so thankful you're still alive. The doctors said you barely made it. How about we focus on that?"

He just sighed and looked off from her.

"I know what you need," she purred gently before reaching her left hand under his hospital gown and grabbing a hold of his soft penis.

Pretty lived up to her name, plus, she had a unique body that AK was in love with. Any other time she touched his dick, he was jumping for joy but he just wasn't feeling it, right now. He tried to push her hand away but she strongly resisted.

"Stop, bae! It's been weeks since I sucked this muthafucka!"

She stood up and helped him get all the way in the bed. She was only 5'3, so it wasn't too difficult for her when she started sucking him while standing.

AK's first thought was telling her to leave him alone, but once the warm saliva from her mouth touched his skin, his whole mood changed. He was getting more and more into it as time passed by.

He laid his head on the bed because he was using the muscles in his neck too much and the pain was irritating. He closed his eyes and let Pretty work her magic with those juicy lips of hers.

For a few minutes, all his concerns were nonexistent. Pretty was doing what she did best, rescuing him from himself.

***

Wopp had to shut every trap down and cease all movement in his camp. Everything was on hold including his money, and that didn't sit right with him. The Southside of Atlanta was a fucking circus. He had a lot of heat coming down on him at the moment, and it was overwhelming. The whole situation was getting way out of hand. Pooh Bear changed the game when he shot that video of Quay.

He flew his entire family out of town and advised his Dons to do the same, there were basic war precautions. They even had a string of low-key spots for times like this for the Mobsters, so they wouldn't be sitting ducks in the pond. The opposition would just have to catch them in traffic.

Wopp had the smallest camp in Atlanta. It was a gift, and a curse at the same time because at times like this, he had to call for reinforcements. This time was a little different because he didn't have to do that. Toe-Tag made it clear that this was his beef and told Wopp to stay out of his way, so Wopp and his camp just had to lay low until the smoke cleared.

He was at Mario's condo downtown getting peace of mind, just blowing off some steam with his little homie. Mario played the game while he kept an eye on all the media reports of the Southside shootings from his phone.

"Scooby hit me up right before you came over here, too," Mario said without taking his attention from the game.

Scooby was Wopp's fourth-level Don. He was the muscle be-hind them and had twelve Mobsters who was just thorough as him.

"Okay, and?" Wopp asked without breaking his attention from his phone.

"He wants to jump in the field and help Toe-Tag put in some work."

Wopp looked up from his phone. "I know that man ain't serious. What we gon' do if something happen to him? He not thinking about that part, huh? Of course not! Seem like nobody thinking about the consequences of the shit they do these fucking days!"

By the time he was done with his statement, Mario was staring at him awkwardly. "Just chill, bro. I basically told him the same shit before we got off the phone. How you think this shit gon' play out?"

"It's gon' be alright."

Mario tossed the controller on the glass coffee table. "Don't hit me with that same bullshit you hit the rest of the camp with. You know how we do it."

"I just know it's gon' be one helluva show to watch," Wopp predicted before jumping back into the world of public media.

Malik D. Rice

CHAPTER 13

After tossing all four of the hostages off the cliff Toe-Tag called it a night and retired back to the hood. He didn't go into his condo because he didn't want to hear Shanay's mouth. He went to another apartment that was used for a chill spot for his Mobsters. He put a half-ounce of weed in the air before falling asleep on the couch.

Knock! Knock! Knock! Knock!

Everybody in the living room popped up as if they were never sleep. They had every reason to be as paranoid as they were. Monster went to the door and looked through the peephole, then opened it. Mooski and Gutta walked into the apartment with long faces.

"What the fuck wrong with y'all?" Monster asked sitting on the arm of a couch wiping cold from his eyes.

Mooski inhaled a deep breath and spoke as he exhaled. He told them everything that happened the night before and basically apologized for making the poor choice of pulling over to the McDonald's in the first place.

Maybe it was the apology, but Toe-Tag didn't bother with the scorning he was going to lay on Mooski. He just dismissed him, and everybody else in the room except for Monster.

"Talk to me youngin," Monster insisted after the apartment was clear.

Toe-Tag took his shirt off and adjusted the tennis chains around his neck. "That video got nine million views in a few days, shawty."

"Don't worry about it we gon' get 'em," Monster assured.

"That's not the point. It don't matter about who we kill now. All that matters is that a nigga in my camp, that I'm responsible for was the victim in that video. Shit gon' be real ugly for me shawty. If I get whacked make sure you protect my family, and I want Mazi in my spot."

Monster looked at Toe-Tag disappointedly. "I never heard you sound so pathetic in my life, shawty! You sound like a real *bitch*, right now, bro. I wouldn't give a fuck if Kapo put the hit out on you. We all sliding! They gon' have to whack the whole camp, and they ain't gon' do that. You know why?"

"Because they need us," Toe-Tag answered correctly.

"Exactly! We the ones that set the standards with the murder game out here."

Toe-Tag clenched his teeth as he played a few possible scenarios out in his head, none of them ended well for him. It's like he was destined for hell or jail. Most people claimed they'd go to hell before spending the rest of their lives in jail, but he disagreed. He was useless dead, but at least in prison he could still hustle and provide for his family. He could still be in their lives even it was halfway.

He couldn't help but wonder if this is how Rampage felt after he found out G-Baby was killed on a mission. He didn't confide in anyone before he was whacked, just did a lot of inward thinking like Toe-Tag was doing now.

He wanted to confide in Monster but that wasn't an option. Monster always prided Toe-Tag and Mazi for being so heartless, so Toe-Tag understood why he didn't want to have a sentimental conversation with him. That's just not what they did.

"Where my brother at?" Toe-Tag strategically changed the subject.

"You know that nigga ran to LaKisha's last night."

***

LaKisha made Mazi a home-cooked meal and served it to him in the bed. He showed up at her spot six in the morning looking a hot mess, so he showered and passed out. He had his own apartment but was choosing to sleep in her bed, so she kept her bed pleasurable for him.

She had her own agenda and didn't have time to be falling in love with a thug, but as she sat there watching him eat her breakfast in her bed wearing nothing but briefs, she was cracking under his spell, and she barely knew the man. He wasn't part of the plan.

"You gon' stick around? I have to get ready for work in a few," she stated.

"Nah, I got a few things to handle my damn self," he answered with a mouth full of food.

LaKisha worked as a consultant at a car insurance place on the other side of town. She left earlier than usual, so she could do some light shopping. When she arrived at work, she clocked in then ate her traditional IHOP breakfast at her small, but comfortable desk in the lobby.

She'd been working there for over a year, and they were like a small family at her office, so she was surprised when her supervisor walked out of her office with a new face. It was a stylishly dressed Caribbean woman. "Ladies, and gentlemen! This is your new coworker, Rain Thompson. She will be filling in for Debra while she's on medical leave."

Those sharp facial features and the curly hair sparked memories in LaKisha's brain. She'd seen the lady somewhere recently.

The supervisor showed Rain to her new desk, and everybody went back to work. LaKisha was caught up with all of yesterday's tasks, so she used the extra time to finish her breakfast. All the orange juice she guzzled down after the meal got her bladder moving, so she headed to the bathroom to relieve herself.

"Ohhh, girl, you scared me," she told Rain who was standing there waiting to go in behind her.

Rain smiled brightly. "I'm sorry, I didn't mean to startle you."

"It's alright." She stepped out of the bathroom

"I like your blouse where did you get it from?" asked Rain.

LaKisha looked down at her white polyester blouse. "This thing is oldddd. Ordered it online from Macy's a while back. Where'd you get those lovely heels from?"

Rain looked down at the Dolce and Gabbana heels on her small feet. "My boss gave me these as a gift."

"You must have another boss because Mrs. Mayes don't even believe in designer," LaKisha joked seriously.

"As a matter-of-fact, I do. You might know him. Little short Irish fella with red hair."

LaKisha had a blast from the past. Suddenly memories came flashing back, and she knew exactly where she knew Rain from. She was a federal agent. "Why are you here? Are you crazy?" she whispered urgently. Suddenly her heart started racing, and her breath was short.

"Girl, calm down, it's called going undercover. Nobody's going to know I'm an FBI agent. I have a house set up close to your apartment, so me and you are going to become the best of friends, and you're going to start bringing me around introducing me as your sexy coworker, which I am."

LaKisha shook her head. "That's a bad idea. I told Mr. Chinx to let me handle this my way."

"Well, unfortunately, you're not a professional and can't be fully trusted. On top of that, when you're dealing with Agent Chinx the only way anything's going to get handled is *his* way," Rain informed matter-of-factly before stepping into the bathroom and closing the door behind her.

LaKisha let out the breath she'd been holding, and sort of floated back to her desk. She sat down and stared at her computer screen blankly. She was starting to wonder if she'd made a mistake getting in bed with the feds. They obviously didn't care about her they just wanted their convictions.

She leaned back in her chair, closed her eyes, and started trying to come up with a way out of the sticky situation she'd gotten herself into.

CHAPTER 14

The media currently consisted of a string of terrorist public shootings and the release of Dinero one of the most notorious men in the entire country. His team of lawyers was very effective and worth every million he spent on them. The government couldn't prove anything more than the fact that he was the one that Dilluminati praised, but other than that, they had absolutely nothing. They couldn't tie him to any specific crimes whatsoever.

They continuously ranted on about the danger of having a man with his kind of power walking free on the street and even had a whole campaign fighting against his freedom, but obviously, it wasn't working because it had just been confirmed that he's scheduled for release in a few weeks since it looks like the government is failing to bring forth hardcore evidence. The judge will be forced to drop the charges against him because a trail can't go on without evidence.

2-Tall smiled brightly as he sat in the back of a limo watching the news report on a small television. His little brother was finally coming home where he belonged. He was already sending texts out to his assistants instructing them on what to do in order to have everything laid out for Dinero when he touched down.

He wanted to take a trip to the jail and visit him, but he was an active drug lord and couldn't show his face there. Plus, he had other business to handle. It was time for him to finally meet, George Mendez. The man behind it all.

He was in Texas getting ready to cross the border over into Mexico. Malina wanted to come with him, but George protested and ordered 2-Tall to come alone. It was a meeting for men.

2-Tall couldn't help but wonder if this would be his last trip. George had a notorious history for being the last person someone sees before they come up missing. Some of those people being his own family, so 2-Tall was curious about the whole situation.

After crossing into Mexico, the limo driver stopped at some sort of outdoor strip mall. Everything was being sold from clothes to fruit. The driver got out, walked around, and opened the door for him. He stepped out into the sun wearing a pair of blue cut off True Religion jeans, a white Ralph Lauren tank top, and a pair of high-top Air Force Ones. The only piece of jewelry he wore was his diamond-covered engagement ring. George told him to be casual, so he obliged.

Four rough-looking Hispanic men walked up to him openly carrying automatic weapons in the crowd. "You follow us," the biggest of the four instructed before tossing 2-Tall a black hood. "Put that on."

2-Tall looked down at the hood, and back up at the man. He wasn't comfortable with it, but he wouldn't dare upset George in *any* shape or form, so he pulled the hood over his head. One of the men duct-taped his neck, so he wouldn't be able to take the hood off easily, then grabbed his arm and lead the way.

Three long hours had passed, and they were still on the move. This was his third time waking up from a nap and was starting to think he'd never make it to the destination. It was a long bumpy ride, and he was thankful when the truck finally stopped. He said a silent prayer as they helped him off the truck. Both of his legs was sleep, so he had to stretch for a minute before they started walking.

He smelled and heard moving saltwater in the distance and wondered exactly where they were. He couldn't see a thing through the hood, but it was made so that he could still breathe perfectly. It was custom made.

"We here?" he said as the concrete he walked on turned into sand.

"No, we get on this here boat, and sail the rest of the way," the man holding him answered.

Just like he said, they got on a small wooden rowboat and sailed. They sailed for at least two hours before the boat touched sand again. The hood was removed from 2-Tall's head, and for the first time in five hours he could see and the sun was gone like he expected.

He looked around past the beach they were on and could see that they were on a very small island probably three football fields long in either direction. There was a classic three-story villa in the middle of the island and that's where the four men were now leading him.

About twenty heavily armed men circled the premises stealthy. 2-Tall could easily tell they were professionals, unlike his four escorts. Two of the island guards stopped them halfway to the villa, thanked the escorts for their work, and told 2-Tall to follow them.

The island was beautiful, and the house was a wonderful addition. They walked inside, and the guards handed 2-Tall over to the maids, who then escorted him to George. 2-Tall followed them down the hall to a room with no door that was filled with books and antique statues, George sat in a chair with a thick book on his lap as he read through his Cartier lenses. He looked more like a college professor than a Godfather of a Cartel family.

He was simply dressed in slacks and a button-down silk shirt with graying hair that he obviously wasn't ashamed of because he wore it down to his shoulders. He looked up at 2-Tall who stood frozen in the doorway and studied him like he was just studying the words in the book.

"Have a seat young man," he instructed pointing at a chair a few feet away from him. "I'm sorry for the extreme precautions during the transportation, but any man of importance knows the value of being incognito."

2-Tall sat down and nodded his head in understanding. "No worries, I'm starting to appreciate the value of it myself."

"Why do you think I finally chose to meet with you today?" George asked after placing the book on a white antique granite table.

2-Tall sat up straight and looked George dead in the eyes. "To be honest, sir, I've been trying to come to that conclusion since I got notice of this meeting. But I couldn't come across anything that honestly makes sense. I mean, it took Malina's ex-husband four years to meet you. So, I've been trying to figure out why is it that I'm sitting face-to-face with you, right now."

George was impressed with his answer. "Before you met Malina, did you know her ex-husband's name?"

2-Tall shook his head *no* slowly.

"Do you think he knows your name?" He nodded. "Exactly, you've done more than beat the odds, you're setting records of your own. That and the fact that you're Malina's new eye candy makes you worthy of sitting in front of a man as notorious as myself. You've made one helluva first impression on the world, son."

2-Tall let the words digest. He was a strong believer in fate and never would've known that this is how his life would play out. He was speechless but had to overcome that because this was literally the most important meeting of his life. "Success was never an option for me, but I honestly never meant to make it this far in the game."

"I admire your mindset. Dilluminati is already one of the wealthiest organizations in the country, and that's because money is flowing from the bottom to the top, and back down. Other organizations never see the money after it's sent to the top, but you, you take care of yours, and I admire that. It tells me a lot about your character. For as good as you're doing, it's easy for one to forget your age, but it can't be disregarded because age is important most of the time. Not to say that it applies to you, because it doesn't. You've surprised a lot of people, but it does apply to certain individuals in your organization. Relatively young individuals with a lot of power. That, and drugs is the problem."

2-Tall's eyes squinted slightly. "*Drugs*? What about them?"

"Well, let's say drug abuse. Drug addiction. It's originally for the peasants, not for the kings of the world. Do you know why Malina forbids you from intoxication?"

"I have too much responsibility for a foggy mind."

George smiled. "Yes, any man of wisdom knows the importance of a clear mind. That was another day though. This here is a new day. A world filled with zombies running away from their own reality."

2-Tall couldn't argue. He used to smoke weed to make him feel better, now money did it for him. "That's deep."

"Indeed. You have to go deep to get to the core of anything dissected. The moral of the story is that Dilluminti's successful, but has a lot of improving to do, and your job is to assure that improvement."

"So, you want me to stop the total use of drugs in my organization?"

George shook his head in disappointment. "It would be ideal, but even I know that's impossible. You can enforce the rule for your Godfathers but I wouldn't care if the rest of them fucked goats in the ass on their free time."

"It's done! I don't mean to be rash, or impatient when I ask this, but what exactly do you want from me?" 2-Tall asked as respectfully as possible.

"I'm sure you've been hearing rumors floating around about these being the last of days. Well, they're not complete rumors. In a sense, these are the last days, but I'm not going to get into the specifics of all that. I'm just going to let you in on this little secret. There's not a lot of time left."

"Time left for what?"

George paused dramatically. "For a whole new world, and I have plans that need to be carried out before that new world is formed. War slows up the flow of money, and another street war with your organization will slow those plans of mines down, on top of bringing more heat down on us. It's just not worth it. So, what I want from you, young man, is peace."

2-Tall looked George in those hazel eyes of his and nodded his understanding. He was still digesting George's words. His life was officially a movie, and George was the new director.

Malik D. Rice

CHAPTER 15

"This shit ain't no damn movie! This life we live is really real. This ain't *Grand Theft Auto.* You can't just go out there spazzing and wake up in front of the hospital when it's all over. We got to start moving a lil' more militant around here and taking more time to strategize." Toe-Tag preached as he stood on top of the jungle gym in the back of their hood.

He was holding a meeting for his camp once again. "I'm just gone go ahead and assume the worse. We probably won't see Quay again, and a lot of folks ain't gon' see the niggas we took. This is a war, and in war, you got to lose before you can gain anything." He scanned the hard faces in the crowd. They were an extension of him. They were family, and he promised from that day forward to take better care of all them because, at the end of the day, they were his responsibility. "I know some of y'all blame me for what happened to Quay, and that's cool because I been blaming my damn self lately. But I'm standing right here taking that blame like a man in front of all of y'all. Looking y'all in y'all eyes, admitting the shit. Ain't no-body perfect, but that's on the Four's I'm gon' do better by y'all. Mark my words."

After the meeting was over Toe-Tag walked up to Mooski who leaned on one of his trucks. "What you think?"

Mooski raised an eyebrow. "Think about what?"

"The speech, nigga."

"I mean, you definitely said some real shit. Can't argue with none of it."

Toe-Tag nodded. "Aye, check this out. I know we done grew apart over the past few months since we moved out here, but I'm gon' need you to start sticking close again."

"What?" Mooski looked at him awkwardly. "Where all this comes from."

"It comes from the heart, nigga. Like I said up there, ain't no-body perfect, but you still got some improvements to make, so I'm putting your training wheels back on."

Mooski frowned instantly. "Come on, shawty! Don't do me like this. You gon' take my stripes? I earned this shit man!"

"Yeah, you definitely did, which is why I'm not taking yo' stripes. I'm just taking your say so. You don't make a move unless it comes through me first. Once you show me, you're ready to earn yo' decision-making rights back, I'll give them to you. So, like I said, stay close."

He could feel Mooski's eyes on him as he walked away. He knew, and understood, why Mooski was upset, but it was for the better.

"So, you mean to tell me this eighteen-year-old has all these men brainwashed? That's amazing!" Rain admitted looking down at Toe-Tag through LaKisha's apartment window.

"Girl, get out that window before somebody sees you!" LaKisha spat standing behind her.

Rain turned around with a serious look plastered on her smooth chocolate face. "I'm just your green coworker from the suburbs who's here with you looking out the window at some sexy men. There's nothing suspicious about that unless you make it suspicious. The first rule of this game we play is to remain calm at *all* times. Do you understand me?"

"Yeah, I got it!" LaKisha retorted sassily.

If she didn't fully regret her decision to get involved with the federal government before, she did now. Previously, her top priority was taking Toe-Tag and Monster down for bringing her son into their mess, but now, all she wanted was to climb her way out of the hole she dug for herself before she ended up missing. The feds were definitely underestimating this camp.

***

Rinno popped up on Jasmine at her place unexpectedly. "What I tell you about popping up on a bitch like that? I'm not pretty, right now," she stated sternly as he walked into her apartment.

She had on tight plaid pajamas with her head wrapped in a Gucci scarf. She was cute, but not cute how she wanted to be for him.

"Stop that nonsense, you're always beautiful in my eyes," Rinno assured her as he pulled her into his arms for a loving kiss.

He smelled of his usual Ferragamo cologne, and she inhaled the scent deeply into her nostrils. It seemed to soothe her soul. Everything about him did, but she tried not to show it.

"Whatever." She rolled her eyes. "Is this for me?" she asked referring to the Chanel shopping bags in his hand.

"Yeah. Just a belt, and some perfume I picked up earlier today while I was out."

She stood on her tippy toes to kiss him again. "Thanks, baby! You know you don't have to buy me gifts every time, right?"

"Yeah, I know, but I like the look on your face when you receive them, so I keep bringing them," he retorted smoothly.

She pursed her lips together. "If you were to ever show up without a gift, you'd notice that the look on my face is because of you, and not the gifts."

He couldn't hide the oncoming blush she'd just squeezed out of him. "Where's my little girl?" he asked referring to Karma who he was crazy over already.

"You just missed her. I put her to sleep about twenty minutes ago, but I'll wake her up for you, though."

He shook his head rapidly. "No, don't worry about it. I have a little surprise for her in the car, I'll just give it to her another time. Anyway, I came to talk to you about something very important."

Jasmine tried to lead him to the couch, but he stopped her in her tracks, and kneeled onto one knee, pulling a small black box out of his back pocket.

"Whattt! I know that's not what I think it is, Rinno! Please tell me that's not what I think it is! Oh, Lord, you gon' give me a damn heart attack. Why would you—"

He chuckled softly. "Baby, shut up, and open the box."

She grabbed the box, opened it, and saw a silver key, a house key. "What's this?"

"A key to my house. I want you and Karma to move in with me. There's plenty of room and kids for her to play with and I can have a whole room cleared out for your office space so you can decorate it yourself. And with all the shit going on with Dilluminati, it'll make me feel better."

"That's a big step, Rinno. I don't know about that."

He stood up and held her hand together as he looked down into her eyes. "Listen, all I want is it to see both of you happy."

Jasmine bit down on her lip in deep thought. So much was going through her mind at the moment. "This is so sudden, and over-whelming baby. Just give me some time to think about this."

CHAPTER 16

Kapo went ahead and bought the office he'd been renting all this time. He had his name placed on the door and redecorated the space to his complete liking. He stood at the wall-length window behind his desk, and a few thoughts came across his head, but he would have to save them for later because his guest was entering his office.

He continued to face the window even as he heard their heels clacking on his hardwood floor. He waited until they got close enough before turning around to greet them face-to-face for the first time.

"Mayor Spring, it's a pleasure to finally meet you face-to-face." He walked around his desk to shake her hand respectfully.

Mayor Spring was a powerful, middle-aged, African American woman that loved the city of Atlanta so much, she decided to make it her responsibility. Under normal circumstances, she wouldn't risk being seen in the presence of an underworld mob boss, but these weren't regular circumstances. She'd learned over the past year of observation that Dilluminati isn't your average organization. They were small in numbers, but they were extremist in good and bad ways.

"I'm sure you know Mr. Tall had this meeting set up between us," she started after helping herself to a seat in front of his desk.

He walked back around his desk and followed suit. "Yes, I do. What I don't know is why you agreed? You never struck me as the type to attend a meeting under the radar."

"There's a lot of things the public doesn't know about me. But that's irrelevant at this point. This meeting isn't about me, it's about Dilluminati. The last war you guys were involved in ended up being recorded as one of the most ruthless street wars the city of Atlanta has ever seen. That was only less than a year ago. I can't afford another one of those wars, right now, Mr. Kapo. So, I'm here asking you, what can I offer you to put an end to this madness?"

Kapo sat up in his chair and adjusted his tie while giving her an odd look. "I've met with a handful of officials and the terms of those agreements always end with me giving them something. I never thought about receiving anything."

"Well, I'm oblivious to whoever you've dealt with in the past. Me personally, I have a lot to give."

"Understood, but unfortunately, I can't do anything right now. Before a war can be stopped you have to let a little bloodshed first so the soldiers won't feel like they're being cheated."

Now she was looking at him awkwardly. "You're the first underworld boss I've ran into that acknowledged their soldiers. It's like their opinion actually matters to you."

"Many leaders these days are starting to forget the fact that soldiers are the root of every organization. Me, personally, I appreciate mine, and I show them that appreciation as much as possible."

The meeting went on for another twenty minutes, and after it was over, there was a mutual understanding, and respect between them. They'd become good associates over time.

***

Spider was a second-level Don in Pablo's camp and took it upon himself to call a meeting between the rest of the Dons in the camp, all the Dons except Toe-Tag.

The meeting took place at his two-story house out in Douglasville, Georgia. He was good friends with Papa and Purp so he felt comfortable talking to them about his concerns.

"Them niggas out of control. They gon' end up getting us all fucked up. Every time, every time some shit happens! Them niggas be the cause," Spider informed heatedly.

Papa stood up against the wall while Spider and Purp sat in different chairs. "Okay, this is a meeting concerning Toe-Tag and his camp, right?" Spider nodded. "Then why didn't you include him in this meeting?" Papa asked with a raised eyebrow.

Spider opened his mouth, then closed it back. "I don't know."

"Yes!" Papa nodded his head knowingly. "You do know. You were scared of how he would've reacted if you spoke those same words to his face."

Spider's face crumbled in disagreement.

"Come on, Spider. That's the only logical explanation. And guess what? I don't even blame you for it. But unfortunately for you, I'm in cahoots with Toe-Tag. If I'm not mistaken you have personal ties with Toe-Tag as well right, Purp?" Purp nodded slowly. "See, you really jumped the gun. You thought that you could form an alliance against a man that's already many steps ahead of you. That's what makes him so dangerous. A killer with a brain is someone you just don't fuck with," Papa informed matter-of-factly. He was disappointed with Spider's poor attempt at deceit.

Spider sat there with his eyes on the ground, and his teeth clenched. He was too angry and embarrassed to think of a savvy comeback to save face.

Papa exchanged a look with Purp before continuing. "What's your purpose behind this meeting anyway?"

"It's not like I was trying to get him whacked, or nothing like that. I just wanted to make him sit down somewhere, so a nigga won't lose no more money," Spider admitted.

"You ain't the only one losing money. But you don't see me going behind Toe-Tag's back calling secret meetings and shit," Purp said speaking for the first time that evening. He hadn't been feeling too well lately.

Papa nodded his understandingly. "Exactly, Toe-Tag would've respected it if you would've approached him face-to-face, but I'll make sure he doesn't find out about this meeting because you might pop up missing behind it."

"So, what am I supposed to do? Just sit back while I lose money?" Spider asked.

"That's the ideal thing to do. War is inevitable, and if anybody was to put an end to it, it definitely wouldn't be us. Masio couldn't even stop him, bro. Use your head, in situations like this, dealing with niggas like Toe-Tag you just got to let shit run its course until further notice. Now, I'm about to call some strippers up, so this meeting won't look suspect."

Malik D. Rice

CHAPTER 17

It's been ten days since the video of Quay's famous torture was presented to the world. Crips and Dinero Guys all around the city were going at it like dogs in one huge cage. There were losses taken on both sides, but they weren't the only ones taking losses. The community was losing as well. They were losing their sense of security, and it scared many of them. Nowhere felt safe.

Nobody really felt safe, but Freddy was one of those few individuals that believed he was actually untouchable which is why he was out driving one of his favorite toys, a peach-colored 2014 Jaguar he received last year as a birthday present. The beautiful Somalian woman that sat in the passenger's seat next to him was the giver of that gift. Her name was, Yanni. She was a very important fashion stylist overseas that he met by chance on a cruise. She agreed to one date with him, and it went well, so she made it her business to link with him every time she traveled to the states.

They were riding down Peachtree Avenue when Yanni informed him that she had to use the restroom, so he pulled into a plaza, and stopped in front of a burger joint. "This place is pretty clean. I ate here a few times, but I could take you to my condo around the corner. It'll only take like ten minutes," he informed.

She answered his question by getting out of the car and rushing inside to relieve herself.

"Guess not," he joked as he stepped out the car and walked inside behind her.

The restaurant wasn't small, it actually had a little size to it, so Freddy scanned the crowd as he walked towards the bathroom. He stood there waiting for Yanni when a small young woman exited the ladies room with a blue bandana tied stylishly around her head. She looked at Freddy hungrily and scanned him up and down. When she got to his neck and saw his DG tattoo, the expression in her eyes changed from interest to caution.

Freddy watched as she rushed away fumbling in her purse for her phone. "Shit!" he spat angrily.

He knocked on the ladies room door. "Yanni, Hurry up! We got to go now!"

"Coming!" she yelled from inside.

He sent a text of his own and when he looked up, he faced the small barrel of a .25 handgun. It was then that he realized the woman wasn't reaching for a phone, she was reaching for a gun, and he had underestimated her because she was a woman.

He put both hands up out of instinct. "Look, lil' mamma, I can make you rich! Just spare me, and I'll make you a rich woman! That's on the Four's!"

A lady coming out of the bathroom started screaming when she saw the gun in her hand and ran to the dining area alerting people of the situation.

"If I spare you, I won't live to spend that money."

"Look at all these witnesses looking at us, right now. I know you're smarter than that, shawty!" He tried his best to persuade her from shooting him.

Pop! Pop! Pop! Pop! She pumped four small bullets into his chest with no hesitation. They sounded like a string of firecrackers going off. "Obviously, you don't know me," she retorted before snatching the car keys out of his hand and strolling out of the restaurant without a care in the world.

***

Shanay popped up on Jasmine's doorstep with a sleeping Lil' Tee in her arms and tears in her eyes. Jasmine answered with a towel wrapped around her wet body. "My bad girl, I was in the shower. What's wrong? Come in!" She stepped aside, so Shanay could walk inside.

Shanay laid Lil' Tee on Jasmine's bed then came back out to the living room to talk to her friend.

"He was doing so good, girl," Shanay informed trying to pull herself together, so she could talk properly. "I mean, he was really getting himself together, and I was so proud of him. I believed him when he told me he would always put his family first, but this man done broke my heart for the last time girl! Every fucking time them streets go to calling, he says fuck everything, including us and go running."

Jasmine shook her head in disappointment. "Damn, girl. I know exactly how you feel, too. You scared you gon' lose him to them streets, huh?"

Shanay nodded while wiping the new tears off her face.

"Yeah, I know. That's exactly what I went through with Rampage's crazy ass. It took me a long while but you know what I learned about niggas like that, girl?"

"What?" For some reason, Shanay knew she needed to hear what Jasmine was about to say.

"They can never belong to you because they're the property of the Devil, and he's going to call for them when it's time."

Malik D. Rice

CHAPTER 18

Right after Freddy was gunned down, a high-ranking member of the Crip nation was brutally executed in front of his mother and three kids the very next day. These were dark times for the city of Atlanta. The murder and missing persons rate was through the roof.

LaKisha was worried about her son and was having a hard time talking sense into his head. "I told your lil' ass to stay in the house, Q! You running around with these killers like the shit's a joke! You wasn't laughing that night you came in my room crying!" she spat standing over him while he laid in his bed on his phone.

He moved the phone out of his face and looked up at her for the first time during the conversation. "I told you not to bring that up!"

"Boy, I don't care about you mugging me. I'm not scared of you! Now, you need to stay your lil' ass in this house like I said."

He sighed and sat up on his bed. "Ma, I wasn't even on no mission last night. I was with Mazi last night. We went to the shooting range man, it's mandatory."

"Stay the *fuck* in this house, boy! Try me if you want to! I'm gon' have a talk with Mazi, too."

She stormed out of his room and he slammed the door behind her. "Slam another door in here, and I'm gon' slam your head through the wall!" her voice boomed through the small apartment.

She went into her room, slammed the door, and plopped down on her bed with her face buried into the mattress. Her eyes were closed, but images of Mazi popped up in her head. The prime reason for her dealing with him in the first place was to get closer to Toe-Tag without looking suspicious. To draw herself deeper into their world, but she never considered the fact that she'd actually catch feelings for the man.

As sweet as he was to her, she knew how vicious he could be. She would never forget the havoc he wrecked on the neighborhood before he went to jail all those years ago. She was in over her head, and she suddenly knew what she had to do in order to make it right.

***

For Dreek the hood felt different with Quay gone. He was taking the loss of his friend hard, and like a lot of other Monsters in the camp, he blamed Toe-Tag for it. Since the incident with Quay, he'd been keeping his distance from everyone but the mobsters up under his command. Shit just wasn't the same anymore, and he didn't feel the love in the camp anymore. Shit was slime, it was cutthroat.

He had just finished paying a visit to both of Quay's baby mothers. Now he was in Quay's mother's apartment with her, and his big sister, Monique sitting across from him.

"Y'all know Quay was my nigga and we was real close. I know y'all probably done heard it a thousand times already, and don't want to hear it again, but I got to let y'all know how sorry I am for what happened to him."

Monique nodded while leaning into her mother's shoulder as she held her. "Quay never said anything bad about you," Monique admitted with a weak voice.

Dreek nodded. "I just want to ask, did anybody other than me come by to talk to y'all?"

"People catch us in passing, and call our phones, but other than that not really. Toe-Tag popped up on my doorstep a few days ago trying to give me a bag full of money, but I slammed the door in his face," Quay's mother informed.

"Why did you turn down the money?" asked Quay.

"Because I know what he did. He sent my son on that suicide mission, and I'll never forgive him for it."

Dreek licked his chapped lips. He felt the same way, but couldn't express himself as outwardly as her for obvious reasons. "Like y'all said, Quay never said anything bad about me, so I'm gon' need y'all to do me a favor." He grabbed the Louis Vuitton book bag off the floor beside him, reached inside, and pulled out $30,000 in bundled bills. "Please accept this to help out. If y'all need anything else, y'all can just come to me personally."

CHAPTER 19

Toe-Tag was immediately summoned by Kapo which wasn't the least bit surprising to him. It actually took longer than he thought. Kapo gave him the address to his office building and had one of his guards escort him upstairs to the office while Mazi and Monster waited for him in the garage in the truck. They got off the elevator on the 40th floor and stepped out into the hallway. There were only six mega offices on the whole floor, and Kapo's could be easily noticed by the security detail stationed right outside the door.

Although Toe-Tag was supposed to be considered family, he was still patted down and relieved of his gun before being allowed to enter the office. He walked past the threshold and stopped in his tracks once he was in the office. He was beyond impressed. He'd never seen an office like this before.

"I see you've finally found your way. Come take a seat," Kapo greeted from behind his desk.

Toe-Tag continued across the big floor and took a seat in one of the chairs. "Most people got candy and shit on their desk for their guests."

"I'm not most people," Kapo countered. "You should know that by now."

"How you holding up old school? You looking a lil' better these days, like you finally stopped stressing," Toe-Tag observed.

Kapo wanted to hate Toe-Tag so badly but couldn't bring himself to do it. It wasn't his fault that Kandice was dead. Vonte didn't really give him much of a choice. When he looked at Toe-Tag he saw traces of Rampage. It was like Rampage was living through him in a way. He really just wanted to see Toe-Tag prosper just like he did with Rampage, but they were definitely hard to deal with most of the time.

"You know you're probably the only Don in all of Dilluminati that gets to enjoy the privilege of reporting directly to their Godfather, but of course you take that for granted like everything else in your life."

Toe-Tag sighed throwing his hand's up in the air. "What I do now? This one ain't even on me. They started this shit. I'm just trying to finish it."

"You're wrong. This one is on you because Quay kidnapped her little brother first, and you're responsible for Quay. I know Quay's the one that pulled the trigger on my daughter, so I really don't give a fuck about him, but politics are politics. I got to make it look like I'm doing my job."

Toe-Tag gave him a sideways look. "What's that supposed to mean?"

"It means that you're supposed to get whacked for the screw-up, but unlike Rampage, I'm giving you another chance."

***

Later that night, Toe-Tag was alone in his condo lying on the living room floor looking up at the ceiling. He kept reflecting on Kapo's words about him taking everything for granted, and him making the same mistake as Rampage. He gave his Mafiosos too much free will, and just like Rampage it fired back on him, but he came out better than his predecessor. Fortunately, he faced a better judge than Rampage.

He basically ended up with a slap on the wrist. Kapo demanded that he pay four payments of $40,000 before the year was over with for his punishment. It would definitely put a dent in his pockets, but Toe-Tag was definitely grateful for the leniency, so he would pay the fines with no problem. As far as the war was concerned, it was completely over.

Before the meeting with Toe-Tag, Kapo sat with the Godfather over the Rollin 60 Crips in Georgia, and they came to a mutual understanding. The backlash just wasn't worth it. Both sides were taking major losses, so they officially squashed it. Any soldier from either side trying to continue retaliation after that point would face consequences.

At first, Toe-Tag felt that it was some bullshit, but as he laid on the floor gathering his thoughts, he realized nothing good came from death. It was just more and more loss. Enough blood had been shed in Quay's name. It was time for him to rest easy.

"I'm sorry, my nigga. I was just trying to teach you a lesson, but it backfired on me," he said aloud to Quay's spirit.

He suddenly had a strong urge to shove some cocaine up his nose to ease the pain, but he fought the demons. Whenever he felt like this, he thought of Shanay and Lil' Tee, but they were gone. He let her down, too. It seemed like that was the story of his life, letting people down.

***

It was 2:00 a.m. when Jasmine's doorbell rung waking everybody in the apartment including the kids, who began crying instantly.

"Ughhhhh! Who is it mannnn?" Jasmine asked while storming to the door like a bat out of hell.

She got to the door and looked out of the peephole. "Oh, helll no!" She stomped into Karma's room where Shanay was attempting to calm her and Lil' Tee down. "You won't believe who at that door girl!"

Shanay shook her head disappointedly. Jasmine didn't even have to tell her who it was. She handed Karma to Jasmine and made her way to the front door. "How the hell you know I was here? I didn't tell nobody where I was going," she stated through the door.

Toe-Tag had a tracker inside her Benz, her phone, and the necklace around Lil' Tee's neck, but of course, he wasn't about to let her know. "I told you I got eyes everywhere."

She rolled her eyes. "It's late, and I don't feel like talking. Go home, Tee!"

"I'll make Monster kick this door down, right now! Don't test me, shawty!"

"Leave me alone!" Shanay pleaded desperately. She needed time away from him.

He started counting down from four slowly. By the time he got to the number two, Jasmine came running to the door with Karma in her arms. "Bitch, you tripping! You know them crazy-ass niggas ain't playing!" she spat before opening the door for them.

When the door opened Toe-Tag stepped into the apartment with a big smile. "Heyyy, baby!" He leaned in to give her a kiss, but she dodged him.

"What you want?" she asked standing there with her arms folded tapping her foot on the ground.

"I want your lil' black ass back at the spot. You ain't gon' keep leaving me like this."

Jasmine let out a chuckle and walked out of the living room, shaking her head.

Monster and Mooski stood guard outside the door to give them some privacy and Toe-Tag made himself at home by popping a squat on one of the couches.

"You not gon' keep choosing the streets over me, and your son. I told you to lay low, and let the soldiers handle that, but noooo! You had to be Superman and fly headfirst into some shit," she said still standing.

"Come on, bae. Don't do that. You know I ain't have no choice."

"Shut the fuck up with that lame-ass shit, Tee!" she spat irritably. "Who gon' tell you something? Nigga you answer to the fucking Godfather personally! You ain't have to do shit you ain't want to do, and obviously, you wanted to do that."

Toe-Tag took notice of the tears that were forming in her eyes, and the raw pain she was displaying through them. He was causing her more pain than anything, and the fucked up part is that he wasn't doing it purposely. The moral of the story is that she deserved a better man than him.

"You know I love you, right?" he asked genuinely.

She wiped her eyes and stared down at him with more seriousness than she ever had before. She was a woman fed up. "If you love me, Tevin, then let me go! Let me live my life. You can see your son as much as you want, but just free me, please. I don't want to be a slave to you anymore."

That hit him *hard*. For a brief second, he displayed pure agony on his face but quickly recovered like the expert he was. "Bang that, right now and I'll do it."

"What?" she asked with a crumpled face.

"Put that on Tevin Jr that's what you want!" he demanded intensely.

She hesitated, but made a recovery of her own, and put her game face back on. "That's on Tevin Jr that I want you to let me go." She loved Toe-Tag from the bottom of her heart, but she had to love herself more, or she'd never be at peace.

Toe-Tag stood up, walked past her to the door, and walked out. When the door shut, she plopped onto the ground and started sobbing quietly. In a perfect world, she'd be happy, but this was reality, and she was torn. It would take time to heal, but she was determined to find peace and purpose in life.

"Finally got those brats back to sleep," Jasmine informed walking into the living room. She saw Shanay on the floor crying and sat down next to her. "You okay, girl?"

Shanay nodded her head. "Yeah, I did the right thing. I'll be alright over time."

Before Jasmine could respond, Toe-Tag, opened the door abruptly startling both of them. He walked inside with a Versace shopping bag in his hand, dropped it on the floor in front of them, and left without a single word, closing the door behind himself.

Shanay took her eyes off the door and looked down at the bag. She scooted herself up closer to the bag, picked it up, and turned it upside down. Just as she expected, bundles of money fell onto the carpeted floor.

Malik D. Rice

CHAPTER 20

~ 1 month later ~

Dinero had just finished watching the Dilluminati movie for the tenth time in his home theater. The producer did a wonderful job on the motion picture. The main character looked like him for the most part. He was 5'10 with a body full of tattoos and shoulder-length dreads that covered his face. Dinero felt he was just a little darker than him, but he couldn't complain, it was a good replacement.

Before he got locked up last year, Dilluminati was taking off, but it didn't blow up until after he was in a cage. He never intended on his creation to grow into a famous quarter-billion-dollar organization. He started Dilluminati for a select few individuals, but people started hopping onto the bandwagon after DG Rell started rapping.

Being in prison dealing with his notoriety was totally different than being on the street. He felt the praise way more now that he was out. He'd always been overly confident, and very sure of himself, so he didn't expect to be overwhelmed upon his release.

He went inside prison a local crime Lord and came out a famous tycoon with more money and power than he ever imagined obtaining. He'd been out three weeks, and already turned down twenty-one interviews, including the ones they tried to pay him to do. Spike Lee did an interview with him for the movie while he was in prison, and at the end of that interview, he assured Spike Lee that he was a lucky man because he would never do another interview again in his life. He planned on keeping that promise.

His beautiful baby mother, Ladie walked into the theater looking like a 5-foot tall barbie doll with her long and silky purple hair, smooth bright skin, and tattoos. Dinero could have just about any woman he wanted, but she was the one that caught his eye then, and she still caught his eye now.

"You up here watching that damn movie again? Next time we run into Spike I'm going to tell him how much you like the film," she stated in her strong New York accent before taking a seat on his lap.

"I already told him." He kissed her neck passionately. "What's up, though? You put DeeGee to sleep already?" he asked referring to their one-year-old son.

She nodded. "Yeah, he's sleep but I think you might want to go to the garage."

"What?"

"It's a surprise, just go, babe!" she pleaded.

"I'm tired of surprises." Despite his statement, he got up and headed to the garage.

A few minutes later, he was walking into his twelve-car garage looking around in disbelief. Foreign sports cars were being unloaded off a truck and parked in vacant parking spaces in his garage. 2-Tall stood in the middle of it all directing traffic.

"What the fuck is all of this man? I told you no more gifts bro," Dinero stated as he approached his friend.

2-Tall smiled and embraced him. "I heard what you said, but here I am back with more gifts."

"What am I gon' do with all these cars? I still ain't drove the other three you gave me."

2-Tall shrugged. "I don't care what you do with them. Look at them for all I care, but here's eight more for you to look at with those three. Follow me."

Dinero shook his head as he followed his mentor. 2-Tall got in the driver's seat of a Bugatti, and he hopped in the passenger's seat.

"You put this bad boy on somebody's racetrack and you're guaranteed to win you some good money," 2-Tall assured with his hands gripped tightly on the steering wheel.

"I'll keep that in mind. How life treating you, though? You holding up?"

"Yeah, I just make sure all the Godfathers are in line and doing what they supposed to be doing."

Dinero nodded. "It's crazy how I'm the Great Godfather, and I'm only twenty-one. All y'all niggas older than me."

"Shit, you paved the way. Without you, none of this would've been possible. If you would've never came to New York, Rell would've never started rapping, and I would've never met Malina. All this shit begins with you, bro," 2-Tall reminded now leaning back in the comfortable leather seat.

"It be hard for me to believe this shit sometimes. We wasn't supposed to get this big."

"But we did for a reason. It was destined for us lil', bro." 2-Tall reached into the glove box, pulled out a suede pouch, and dropped it on Dinero's lap. "Take a look at that."

Dinero picked the pouch up, untied it, and peeked inside with wide eyes. "Bro, what the fuck is this?"

"If it's not twenty million worth of diamonds, it's right up under it, but you could definitely round it out. I figured instead of giving you a bunch of cash, I'll just give you these instead. Our Florida Godfather got a mean plug on them. So, I been washing my money that way. Cash is on the verge of being worthless, bro."

Dinero was still confused. "What you giving them to me for? You just gave me ten million in foreign accounts on top of all the money I already had. I'm straight, bro. You don't have to keep doing this."

"That's where you're wrong. Everybody paying dues to their Godfathers, and all the Godfathers paying dues to me. After I give the cartel their cut, it's only right that I pay dues to you. My loyalty is always gon' be forever."

Malik D. Rice

CHAPTER 21

Toe-Tag took a trip downtown to Atlantic Station to AK's condo. He'd been discharged from the hospital but was still under health restrictions. He basically just had to get plenty of rest and reframe from too much talking, but of course, he wasn't trying to hear that.

Pretty opened the door so Toe-Tag, Monster, and Mooski could walk in. They found AK on the floor with his shirt off, and his dreads tied up, doing pushups slowly.

"I thought the doctor said no extreme movement. What you call that?" Toe-Tag asked as they walked into the living area.

AK did three more pushups before standing up and greeting them all separately. "About time you came and checked on a nigga," he said in a low and raspy voice.

"You know how this shit go. A nigga been busy, and since Shanay left a nigga, I been going hard in the lab trying to get these cameras rolling for my project."

AK looked at him knowingly. "She'll be back."

"Nah, bro. Even if she wanted to, I wouldn't let her. She stamped that shit and put it on our son. It's over!"

AK took a seat on one of the sofas, and everyone else followed suit. He turned down the music, so he could be heard better. "Probably for the best. You a hard nigga to love."

"I know you ain't talking, nigga! You done scarred every bitch you ever touched," Toe-Tag retorted playfully.

AK chuckled softly and stuck his middle finger up. "We hard to love then. Anyway, I got somebody that's been wanting to talk to you, but I ain't let it happen because you was with Shanay."

"Who?" Monster asked with raised eyebrows before Toe-Tag could.

AK pulled out his phone and showed them a picture of himself with a classy, thick, chocolate vixen.

"Damn! Who's that?" asked Toe-Tag.

"Bro, that's Sapphire's lil' sister! I'm following her on Instagram!" Mooski answered while squinting at the phone.

Toe-Tag racked his brain for recognition. "Sapphire the stripper? That's her little sister?"

Everybody nodded.

***

Quavo flew up Bouldercrest on his four-wheeler trying to clear his mind. He didn't do drugs, and his girlfriend still wasn't trying to come off the pussy, so this was his way to relieve stress. He'd never been put in a tougher position in his young life, but this was his reality and he had to deal with it. He neared the four-way where the Texaco was and crossed the intersection dodging oncoming cars onto Flat Shoals road. His mind was clear as the wind hit his face, he was in the zone.

He thought about the conversation he'd overheard earlier that day. His mother's new friend was a fucking federal agent, and she was cooperating with them. At first, he thought life in prison was his worst nightmare, but this topped that by a long shot. He was so disappointed in her and confused that he was literally torn into pieces. If she was caught, she'd definitely get whacked, and he'd be right behind her for whacking whoever did it. It was a lose-lose situation. He'd never been so anxious about anything before.

He hit the clutch after he passed the three-way on Flat Shoals and roared down the street swerving in and out of traffic on his way toward Moreland Avenue. If only he could speed away from his problems that fast.

***

Rinno was basically royalty but chose not to follow in his father's footsteps by leading the family business. He had a gift for architecture and planned on taking part of his inheritance to eventually start up his own firm. He just wanted to be an honest working family man, and Gilmore accepted that. He had younger sons that could take over the family business by the time he was ready to retire, so Rinno got a pass. They were on the inside tennis court on the West Wing of the family mansion running a game while having their weekly father and son talk.

"At first, it was just the girl and the kid. Now it's a whole other girl and another kid? I don't know about that son," Gilmore informed seriously.

"You don't want me to move out, but you won't let me move people in."

Gilmore ran over two steps and hit the ball over the net expertly. "You did move out to the guest house. That's your domain, and you can move people in, just not four people. Who is this other girl, anyway?"

"Jasmine, Toe-Tag's baby mother. She left him."

Gilmore didn't even attempt to hit the oncoming ball. He just stood there looking at Rinno with his mouth wide open. "Are you serious? You're trying to move Toe-Tag's baby mother here? Are you on drugs, son?"

"You know I'm not on drugs. Jasmine is best friends with Shanay, and they just wanted to keep the kids close, so they could grow up together. I might have to find another place since you won't allow her here," Rinno reasoned.

Gilmore dropped the tennis racket, walked around the net, and grabbed Rinno on the neck. "Listen to me, son. You won't be living under the same roof with her *period*. That could cause bad blood between me and Dilluminati. I just won't have it. You hear me?"

Rinno nodded his head in understanding. He knew what it was when his father spoke in that tone. This was unnegotiable.

Malik D. Rice

CHAPTER 22

After Mooski got back from the visit with AK he left Toe-Tag and headed to his apartment building. He kind of felt weird being sober. Well, he wasn't actually sober, he'd smoked some weed earlier, but he wasn't wired off cocaine, and it had been a while since his nose had been clean. Toe-Tag called himself being a good influence by making him stay clean.

It had been two weeks, he'd already gained eight pounds and started looking a little healthier. People kept telling him how proud they were of him for leaving the powder alone, so he stuck to it. Apparently, no one really liked him when he was on it.

He spotted Babie talking to Nightmare in front of their building. Nightmare stayed in Paradise East. He was one of Turk's favorite soldiers. They all went to school together, so they knew each other but the fact that she was talking to this nigga one-on-one didn't sit right with him, and he'd never been the type to hold his tongue, so he pulled up on them.

The sun had just gone down and they were facing the building, so they couldn't see him approaching up the sidewalk. Babie was laughing at something Nightmare had said when he approached. "What's so funny?" he asked calmly, but firmly, startling them both. Since he'd been sober, he hadn't been extra hyper. He was back to his calm and collected self.

Babie's eyes got big, and her words was stuck, so Nightmare answered for her. "I was just talking to lil' sis about my baby mama, and some shit we going through."

Mooski nodded his head slowly. "That's wassup," he answered before walking off without another word, or glance backward. He walked up the stairs and entered their apartment.

Nightmare brushed him off and tried to continue his story but Babie just wasn't there. Her mind was on Mooski now. The Mooski she was used to would've tried to pick a fight with Nightmare, or her, but he just walked off, something wasn't right.

"I'm sorry, but I got to go. I'll see you around," she informed before walking off.

Nightmare watched her go with a devilish smirk.

Babie walked into the apartment and found Mooski in the kitchen preparing a meal. That was one of the things she loved about him. You couldn't find too many boys her age that actually knew their way around the kitchen.

"That's on Rampage's soul that it's nothing going on between me and Nightmare," she assured truthfully.

He cleaned out the sink so he could season a bag of wings he'd set out earlier. "I said alright, I ain't tripping shawty."

"That's what's fucking me up. The fact that you're not tripping. I mean, even though it's nothing going on between us, you usually would've caused a scene out there."

"Guess a young nigga growing up. I ain't got time for all that. What you want to go with these wings?" She just stood there staring at him. "What?"

"You must got another bitch or something?" she asked accusingly.

He started laughing as he dumped the wings into the sink. "Really, why I got to have another bitch? Because I'm not trying to go through no drama with you?"

She continued to stand there staring at him through squinted eyes. "Ummm-hmmm, whatever! I want fries with my wings please," she informed before heading to their bedroom to call Kamya and see how she was doing.

***

"You're not the nigga with the gun no more. You the nigga with the money now, and the nigga with the money got more problems, and responsibility, than the nigga with the gun," said Papa.

They were sitting on the floor at one of the stash houses counting freshly cooked counterfeit bills with money counters in an empty bedroom. Papa knew all about Handsome, and took a liking to him over time, so he chose to take him up under his wing.

"What about power?" Handsome asked. "We got more power than the nigga with the gun, right?"

106

Papa chuckled. "I left power out on purpose. You know why?"

"Nah, but I'm sure you gon' tell me," he retorted jokingly.

"I left it out of the equation because I can't sit here and honestly say that for sure. I'll use myself and Toe-Tag as an example."

Handsome seemed to start listening harder at the mention of his previous Don which is exactly why Papa used him.

"I got about three times more money than Toe-Tag but that doesn't automatically make me more powerful than him. Don't get me wrong, money is definitely power, but it's deeper than that. You think I'm in cahoots with Toe-Tag because of his wonderful personality?"

Handsome smiled at him devilishly knowing damn well that wasn't the case. Toe-Tag was a total dick and it wasn't a secret. "Hell no!"

"Exactly! It's what you call a strategic alliance. I got personal ties with him because he has balls that I don't and I have money that he doesn't. That plus a more brains but we're both smart enough to know we're more powerful with each other. Unity is the real power."

Handsome nodded his understanding. "I like that. If you don't do nothing else, you gon' keep it real. That's why I fuck with you. Not because you my Don and I want to play up under you. I fuck with you because you done showed me over time that you really care about the Mobsters in your camp. That go a long way with me."

"That's good to hear. You got plenty of potential, lil' bro. Just keep your hand off that gun, and let the shooters do their job. You'll be fine."

Malik D. Rice

CHAPTER 23

Turk's name held super weight in the PDE community, and his opinion held weight as well which is why Killa went out his way to set an urgent meeting up with him. Turk knew all about Killa's grimy ways, so he brought a handful of his most efficient shooters with him to the meeting just in case things just so happened to go South. He had a few slime bones in his body, every real street nigga did, but Killa was a whole Anaconda. He was the only nigga in the streets that people considered to be worse than Vonte and that was saying a lot.

The meeting was set at a strip club on Moreland Avenue called Foxy Lady. Killa spent a lot of his free time there and sometimes handled business there like he was doing now.

Turk and his crew walked right past security at the entrance. They knew who Turk was and knew better than to insult him by trying to search him or his company.

There were only two VIP sections in the small hole in the wall, so it wasn't hard for Turk to find Killa who surprisingly had only two soldiers with him that night.

"I see you traveling light tonight," Turk stated before taking a seat next to Killa on the soft couch.

Killa smiled, showing his teeth that looked extra white against his dark skin. "Had to make sure you was comfortable, Blood. We ain't never had no bad blood between us and I don't want none."

"I hear what you saying but everybody know you don't move unless you delivering bad news, so just let me have it."

Killa picked up a bottle of champagne off the table in front of them and took a few sips from the bottle before responding. "I can't even argue with that right there but I guess it's a first time for everything because this ain't no bad news. Not for you anyway."

"Who the bad news for then?"

"Dilluminati, I need you to cut ties with them, so I can make my move on them suckas."

"Why would I do that?" Turk asked with a raised brow.

"Why wouldn't you? You saw how they did your lil' homie, Quay."

"If it was up to me it would've been done. That's over my head. You know better than me that Dilluminati is mostly protected because of their money, and money makes the world go around. My Godfather not gon' go for it, but I'll still check and see."

"That's all I'm asking."

Turk peeled his eyes away from the chocolate stripper on the stage and looked at Killa curiously. "What's your angle, though? Vonte gon' so who you got it out for now?"

Killa wasn't expecting the question but didn't hesitate to answer. "I don't got it out for none of them niggas. Like you said, Vonte ain't in the picture no more. I'm here on behalf of my Godfather. That bitch ass nigga Spider cut off all dealings with us, so you know how that go."

"That might change the game. Give me a few days, I'll get back with you."

Killa shook Turk's outstretched hand. "Please do because we would hate to retaliate while y'all still got ties, but that don't mean it won't happen."

***

Ronte was one of the most favored gangster rappers in the game because he wasn't out there glorifying the street life. He was revealing it for what it was. All the hardships, pain, and losses that came with being in the game. He encouraged his fans that were living that life to get what they could get and jump out of the game as soon as possible because it was rare that anyone made it out.

The raw painful emotions he felt surging through his body as he stood over, Freddy who laid in a hospital bed looking up at him with tubes hooked up to his body was very real. Freddy had lost a lot of weight during his struggle to get better over the past month. Ronte had always looked up to him like a superhero, so seeing him laid up all frail-looking did something to his mental.

The doctors recently reported Freddy as being stable. It was a battle extracting the small bullets that had traveled through his body upon entrance, but the battle was won, and Freddy was on his way back to health. He'd just have to remain in the hospital for at least another month and take it easy after that, but overall, he was definitely blessed to still be alive.

"You looking good nephew," Freddy admitted in a weak voice while looking up at Ronte who was dressed like the superstar he was. All designer and diamonds.

Ronte bent down to press the *up* button on the remote attached to the bed that raised the upper half of the bed so he could see Freddy better. "You look like shit, man. I can't even lie," he joked seriously.

Freddy let out a short painful laugh. He felt even worse than he looked. "Yeah, I know. It's my fault, though. I was slipping and I underestimated that bitch. That'll never happen again."

"What? The first one or the second."

"Both, I learned a valuable lesson that day," Freddy admitted humbly.

Ronte nodded in agreement. "Don't worry about it, unk. I got word that Dead Shot snatched the bitch up and dropped her in a tub of boiling water."

Freddy cringed at the thought. "Yeah, I heard. He came and told me himself after the deed was done."

"You been doing this shit for a while now. You ain't ever think about hanging it up? I mean, I know you got to be eligible for a retirement plan by now especially after this shit right here."

Freddy laughed again but this time he ignored the pain. "Yeah, right! I'm gon' die on this thrown, nephew. Kapo definitely ain't going for that. He holds me and Masio responsible for him not retiring, and most importantly he holds us responsible for the death of his wife, and daughter."

Ronte mugged making him look exactly like his twin brother. "How the fuck is that?"

"He feels that if we would've let him retire, Kandice would've still been alive, his wife would've never lost her mind, and he would've never had to whack her."

CHAPTER 24

After dealing with the backlash from the war, Kapo decided it was time for a much-needed vacation. He was probably one of the hardest working Godfathers Dilluminati had. At first, he was submerged in his work for the sake of his sanity. It was a good way to keep his mind off his family, but now, things were quite different. Not only was Mina in the picture, but an expansion of himself. A child at this point in his life was probably the best thing for him. He needed someone to love. Someone to soften his hardened heart because he didn't like the soulless individual he was quickly becoming.

Mina had decided on a cruise for their vacation, so they could enjoy the last of the beautiful summer weather. Kapo agreed that a vacation on the sea was a great idea. To take a break from civilization, but he disagreed onboarding a public cruise ship. He had to remind her that she wasn't a regular citizen anymore. That child in her stomach certified her as an elite superior and elite superiors didn't take vacations on public cruise ships, they sailed on private yachts, so Kapo set it all up.

He called up a new friend of his who owned a fleet of mega yachts and rented one for their vacation right in front of her. They were on the spacious balcony of Kapo's biggest downtown condo thirty stories in the sky. It wasn't just his anymore, it was theirs until he could find the perfect location to have a mansion built for them to raise their family.

Mina sat upright on the Italian leather sofa that was facing the breathtaking view down below, but she didn't pay it any attention, she was looking down at, Kapo who laid across the sofa with his head resting on her lap.

"I would've never in a million years imagined myself with a man like you, but it's weird because you make me so happy when you're not even happy yourself."

Kapo sighed as he closed his eyes not wanting to look into hers at the moment. "Don't start that shit, Mina. As long as you're happy, that's all that matters. Don't worry about me, I'll be fine."

"That's *so* not fair. Why shouldn't your happiness matter? Because you're a man? That's a barrel of bullshit! You deserve the same happiness you make me feel. Hopefully, this baby will do it for you."

He turned his head and kissed her growing stomach. "We gon' be straight. It's all gon' work out for the best."

"I think I'm falling in love with you, and I'm not even afraid," she admitted suddenly.

He finally looked up into her eyes and could easily see that she was telling the truth. Unlike him, she didn't have any barriers up over her soul. It softened him a little knowing that he had someone who genuinely cared about him the way she did, but he was too torn to match her affection.

He couldn't understand how she was loving him enough for both of them. That was telling him all he needed to know about her, but despite the fact, he still couldn't bring himself to even try to take his guard down. He was still bleeding from his wounds, so he couldn't take the bandages off just yet.

"Just work with me, babe, I need time. Hopefully one day I'll be able to enjoy you as much as you enjoy me."

***

Being the top Don made Papa responsible for making sure the meetings amongst the other Dons continued. This meeting wouldn't be in public because everything wasn't running smooth. They had issues to discuss, so he set the meeting to take place at the DG chill spot off Covington Highway.

He sat at the head of the oval table in the conference room with Spider and Toe-Tag on either side. They were waiting on, Purp who had just walked into the room looking rugged surprising all three of his peers. Purp was known for his spectacular appearance, so him having an off day was definitely something new for them.

"What the hell wrong with you, shawty?" Toe-Tag asked with wide eyes.

Purp plopped down in his chair at the other end of the table with a huff. "What it look like, nigga? I'm sick. Y'all lucky I showed up. Now let's get this shit over with."

"Y'all heard, Mr. Grumpy!" Papa started. "This is an official meeting for the Dons of our camp. Anything you got to say, let it be said. You know something that you think everyone should know, let it be known."

Toe-Tag cleared his throat. "I'll go first, y'all know what I got going on with this new project. I'm holding auditions soon, so let y'all Mobsters know. I need as many DG officials in the project as possible. Especially you, Purp, I'm gon' need a few of them freak hoes you got on standby."

Everyone nodded enthusiastically. It was a blessing that Toe-Tag was being positive, and not trying to paint the streets red, so they were all for it and would definitely support him *any* way possible.

"I been getting threats from the G-Shine Bloods over the lil' clean up I did not too long ago," Spider admitted seriously while looking around the table at the different expressions.

Toe-Tag leaned in closer to the table. "Hold on, say that again for me. I think I heard that wrong."

"I cut them niggas off," Spider replied matter-of-factly.

"God damnnnnn, Spiderrr!" Toe-Tag roared as he abruptly banged down on the table with both fists startling everyone in the room. He went from zero to one hundred very fast.

"What I do? It ain't like they was the only ones. I cut ties with a few organizations. I'm not obligated to do business with nobody. Especially niggas that don't fuck with us anyway." Spider stated matter-of-factly.

Toe-Tag wanted to rip Spider's tongue out for speaking that nonsense to him. "I still can't see why Kapo made your stupid ass a Don. Use yo' head, nigga. It ain't no secret that they don't like us, and that rookie ass move you just pulled gon' give them a reason to do what they been wanting to do anyway."

"Man fuck all that. I'm not doing business with no niggas that don't got my best interest at heart."

Toe-Tag tried his hardest to calm himself down. He leaned back in his seat, closed his eyes, and took a series of deep breaths. When he opened his eyes, everyone was looking at him waiting to see what he was going to do or say, next. "Listen, stop thinking with yo' emotions for a minute, and use your head. Them folks got three times our numbers, and they on the same side of town as us. How many shooters you got in your camp? I bet you it's no more than ten that can stand the kind of pressure they gon' apply. Purp don't got none, and Papa only got Handsome. I'm down to thirty-one, and you can cut that number in half if you take out my Baby Mobsters. Now you tell me if you think that war is worth your pride."

Spider thought about it, but obviously, he was still thinking with his emotions. "I don't know, Toe-Tag. I might be tripping, but it sounds to me like you scared."

The rational part of Toe-Tag's brain went into a temporary coma as he popped up out of his seat with impressive speed, jumped onto the table, and dropped down onto his ass, but not before stretching his legs out striking Spider in the torso with powerful force causing him to fall backward out of his seat, crashing onto the floor.

Papa was up out of his seat trying to hold Toe-Tag back away from, Spider who laid on the ground with wide eyes gasping for air. "Chill, bro!"

"Get the fuck off me!" Toe-Tag spat as he pushed Papa off him and stood onto his feet in the same motion.

Spider was attempting to get up onto his feet when Toe-Tag kicked him in the stomach causing him to crumble back to the ground in more pain. "Ahhhh, chill!"

Toe-Tag grabbed a fist-full of his shirt and pinned him on the ground. He leaned in very close so Spider didn't miss a word he had to say, "I ain't scared of *nobody,* nigga! I'm just smart enough to know that a war with them gon' do real damage! Next time you come out your mouth sideways at me, I'm gon' cut your tongue out, and make you swallow that muthafucka! Now, this what you gon' do. You gon' rearrange that agreement you had with them, and you gon' continue dealing with them! You hear me?"

"Y-yeahhh, I hear you!"

"Good," Toe-Tag stated as he released Spider, then helped him up.

Papa decided that was enough for one day and cut the meeting short.

Malik D. Rice

CHAPTER 25

When Shanay left Toe-Tag, she left her house key on the dining room table, and Toe-Tag recently gave that spare key to, Mazi just in case he ever needed it. It was the middle of the night, so Mazi didn't bother to knock or ring the doorbell, he just simply let himself in. The apartment was dark, but he knew his way around, and swiftly maneuvered his way to Toe-Tag's room.

The door was halfway open, so he pushed it open the rest of the way causing it to creak a little, and that little creak was all it took.

"What the fuck?" Toe-Tag spat as he quickly rolled over and outstretched his arm with his Glock 18 in it.

"Boy, you better not shoot me! This Mazi, nigga!" he informed urgently with his hands up knowing full well how lethal his little brother's trigger-finger had become.

Vocal recognition set in, so Toe-Tag lowered his arm, and flopped back down onto the bed with a huff. "Shit, man, I almost knocked yo' top off."

"I see. Bet you I won't sneak up on you no more." Mazi informed before turning on the light and taking a seat on the small couch along the wall facing the bed.

"Wassup, who done died now?" asked Toe-Tag as he sat up on the edge of the bed trying to shake the sleep off.

"Nobody got whacked. I came over here for something else."

Toe-Tag looked at him expectantly. "You waiting on me to grow a beard or something? Spit it out, bro," he urged strongly. He was ready to go back to sleep.

For the first time in history, Mazi was timid around his younger brother, and it was for good reason. "It's about Kandice."

***

"I want you to tell Toe-Tag that I strictly prohibited Rinno from living under the same roof as Shanay. His relationship with Jasmine is one thing, but I won't chance a potential conflict with one of my own friends," Gilmore assured Monster.

They were in Gilmore's lobby shooting their usual game of pool, and politicking.

"Man, Toe-Tag got so much shit on his plate right now, I doubt he worried about that girl. These are delicate times for Dilluminati, right now and you know Dinero out of jail now, so niggas walking on eggshells.

"He might be worried about her in the future. Either way, I'm still prohibiting it as a sign of respect," Gilmore informed, lining up the winning shot. He pumped the pool stick shooting the 8-ball into the middle pocket. "That's three games in a row, my friend!"

Monster tossed his pool stick onto the table. "Toe-Tag wanted me to ask if you had a few marksmen to spare if the need ever occurred?"

Gilmore dropped his stick on the table and led the way to the bar. He sat on one of the barstools and ordered two shots of Vodka from a beautiful half-naked Armenian bartender. "You guys in trouble?" he asked with a raised eyebrow.

"Nah, we good right now, but let's just say that we in a small boat with a pack of sharks circling around us. We just need to be prepared if those sharks decide to tip the boat over into the water."

The bartender returned with the shots and placed one in front of each of them. "Of course, I have thirty men in Georgia and can fly more in if needed."

Monster took his shot in one swallow and slammed the tiny glass back down on the table with a sour face. "That's what I like to hear, G!" he said before ordering two more shots.

***

After laying up in his bed all night reflecting on the discussion he had with Mazi. Toe-Tag finally drifted off back to sleep around seven in the morning only to be awakened by his door a few short hours later. Just like every other time he was torn out of good sleep, he jumped up with his gun in hand.

"Ooowww, boy this better be good!" he growled as he made his way through the condo on his way to the front door.

He checked the peephole and saw Dreek so he opened the door. "Why you ringing my doorbell like you done lost your mind?"

"They just snatched up Mooski!" he informed urgently. He was out of breath from running across the neighborhood to Toe-Tag's building.

Toe-Tag's eyes got big as his adrenaline began to rise automatically. "Who, Crips?"

Dreek shook his head. "Nah, bro, the police! You know he had that warrant for the home invasion and some more shit. They at his apartment now tearing that bitch up while he in the back on one of them cars."

Toe-Tag had heard enough, he took off running towards Mooski's building. Dreek closed his door that Toe-Tag left open and took off running behind him.

"Say, Tee! Sayyyy, Teeeee!" Dreek shouted as loud as his tired lungs would allow.

Toe-Tag looked back without stopping. "What man?" The irritation in his voice was very thick.

"Look in yo' hand, nigga!" Dreek pointed out as they neared Mooski's building that was surrounded by both marked, and unmarked, police cars.

Toe-Tag looked down in his right hand with wide eyes. He'd been so zoned out he forgot his gun was in his hand. He jogged back to Dreek and handed him the gun. "Go put that away and pull back up," he instructed before taking back off towards the circus ahead.

Mooski sat in the back of the police cruiser with his hands cuffed behind his back reflecting on his short life. He'd done a lot in the short amount of time that he'd been in the game, but at the same time, he was still young. He still had so much life to live, but it looked like he'd be living it behind bars now. Just that fast, his whole life was flipped upside down.

He looked out the window of the car and saw the crowd of people gathered around watching the situation unfold. They just weren't any ole people, though. They were his family, people he'd known his whole life that he wouldn't see again for a very long time.

He saw Babie leaning on ZyAsia's shoulder crying her little eyes out. He couldn't even bring himself to feel any type of way about it because he knew it wouldn't be any longer than four days before she was leaning on some niggas shoulder for *comfort*. It was part of the game, so he just sucked it up, and did his best to cope with reality.

The next thing he saw made him burst out into laughter despite the radical situation. Toe-Tag was running toward the police car with nothing but basketball shorts on. The nigga was barefoot, and all.

When he got to the car his frown got meaner. "What the fuck you laughing at?"

"You, nigga. Where your shoes at?"

Toe-Tag squinted his eyes. "All this shit going on and you worried about my feet, nigga? Get your head in the game. What all you got up there?"

Mooski's smile faded immediately as he thought about all the guns, drugs, and money he had stashed throughout the apartment. He looked up at Toe-Tag with wide eyes while exhaling deeply and shaking his head.

He didn't have to say a word, Toe-Tag knew exactly what he meant.

"Hey, get away from that car!" A white officer ordered, pointing his gun at Toe-Tag getting the attention of other officers who were outside and drew their weapons as well.

They rushed over to remove Toe-Tag, but he was smart enough to back away from the car himself. "Don't worry about it, lil' bro! I'm gon' get you up out of there!" he promised as he faded back toward the rest of the crowd.

Mooski heard what he was saying, but he didn't feel it. He knew he'd never touch the streets again. They could put him away forever with just the two dirty guns he had stashed in the kitchen cabinet, it was game over for him.

CHAPTER 26

Later that evening, Toe-Tag had to attend another meeting with the Dons of his camp. He didn't feel like it, but Papa basically begged him to come. He really wasn't in the mood, so he told them they could have the meeting at his place. A few hours later, they were there.

Papa spoke up first as usual, "This not an official meeting. It's just an emergency meeting that needed to be called."

"Who called it?" asked an impatient Toe-Tag.

Purp stood slowly and looked down at each of them separately. He still looked less than himself, and his overall energy was different. "I know y'all got shit going on, and I'm sorry for taking up y'all time. I got an issue that I was gon' address at the last meeting, but didn't get the chance," he informed, looking over at Spider.

"What you looking at me for? He the one that jumped on me!" Spider stated defensively.

"Shut up, Spider!" Papa ordered firmly before motioning for Purp to continue.

Purp waited for the tension to leave the room before continuing. "What I'm about to tell y'all gon' affect a lot of lives, so y'all need to listen carefully. When I was young, my uncle was the one that sold me the game on pimping hoes. I looked up to him and listened to everything he ever taught me, but the problem is that I only applied most of it."

He bent down, reached into his Goyard bag on the floor, and came out with a small purple .380 that he politely placed on the table.

"What the fuck is that for?" Toe-Tag asked with a raised brow.

"That—that's for y'all if one of y'all decide to put one in my head after I tell y'all what I'm about to tell y'all."

Toe-Tag leaned forward on the couch with a curious expression. The suspense was killing him. "You need to hurry the fuck up and say what you got to say."

"The doctor told me this morning that I had AIDS for the past two years," Purp admitted hurtfully.

Every eye and mouth in the room was open as wide as they could go except for Purp's. The other Dons sat there frozen in shock trying to digest the news. Purp had made an understatement earlier when he said that the news would affect a lot of people. If he had the disease for two whole years, he'd probably upped the AIDS rate in Georgia at least forty percent. He had about forty hoes selling pussy for him. Between the forty of those prostitutes, they probably serviced nearly two-thousand men. Out of those two-thousand men, at least seven-hundred was stupid enough to lay with one of those women unprotected.

The worst part was that Purp fucked every last one of his hoes unprotected while they were still *fresh* before he ever put them on the stroll, and every last one of those hoes pussy-bumped with each other, so it was definitely safe to say that there was *a lot* of AIDS floating around very close to home.

"Yeah, you was right," Toe-Tag admitted. "That news right there does change the game."

***

Ronte's manager got in touch with Kapo's assistant and arranged a meeting between them. Ronte invited Kapo to join him backstage at a show he was doing in Atlanta, but Kapo declined and scheduled for the meeting to take place at his office before the show. The only reason Kapo agreed to the meeting was because he was very curious as to why Ronte would want to have a sit down with him. He sat behind his desk rocking a perfect fitting Alexander McQueen suit as he watched Ronte stroll across his floor with the confidence of any other Grammy award-winning superstar.

Ronte helped himself to a seat and didn't waste anytime on greetings, "We need to talk."

"That's obvious," Kapo retorted matter-of-factly. "What we have to talk about is the mystery."

"I'm here for my uncle, Freddy."

"He's dead?" Kapo asked dryly indicating he wouldn't care if he was, or not.

Ronte sat up in the chair and ran a hand down his face. He knew Kapo didn't like him because he was Vonte's brother, and he didn't like Kapo either, but he had to hold his cool and remember that he was there for his uncle. "No, he's not dead, but I came to ask you for a favor man-to-man."

All Kapo could think about was Vonte as he sat there and stared at Ronte. Although Ronte had never done anything to him, he was still guilty by association. "What is it?" he asked even though he knew he'd decline anyway.

"I got a whole ticket for you to give Freddy a pass to retire," Ronte informed seriously.

That caught Kapo's attention. "You willing to pay me a million dollars of your own money for that?"

"Yeah, but just don't tell him about this meeting because he his pride gon' be hurt."

Kapo smiled because he had learned something new. Ronte was nothing at all like his brother on the inside. "Freddy lucky to have family like you in his life. But to answer your question, unfortunately, I can't do that. I'm afraid Freddy's doomed with the same fate as myself. He gon' be in the game until he takes his last breath."

Malik D. Rice

CHAPTER 27

~ 2 Months Later ~

Dinero figured if he could spend all that time in a cell that was four times smaller than the closet attached to his bedroom, he could spend the majority of the rest of his life in his upstate mansion in New York. He never meant to become a celebrity, but what he started ended up being bigger than life itself, and when that many made-men praised you, the rest of the world followed suit.

Dinero sat between Ladie's legs while she thickened his dreads by twisting them together in pairs of twos. 2-Tall sat on a very comfortable loveseat with his hands wrapped around Malina's small waist as she sat on his lap. The 1998 classic movie *Belly* played on the gigantic 75-inch screen that was plastered on the wall. They were just chilling.

2-Tall understood why Dinero was holed up inside his residence. If he was in the same position, he would've been the same way, so he made it a must to visit his nigga at least twice a month.

Dinero wasn't watching the movie, he was studying 2-Tall, and Malina. Malina was the best thing that ever happened to Dilluminati, and 2-Tall was the one that reeled her in, so Dinero would always be indebted to him whether he accepted it, or not.

2-Tall felt eyes on him and shifted his glance toward Dinero. "What you looking at, lil' nigga? See something you like? You not in jail no more, bro," he joked.

"Shut the fuck up!" Dinero barked as he picked up the remote and threw it at 2-Tall. As soon as the remote left his hand, he wished he could get it back.

Dinero's eyes got bigger than his ego and his jaw had dropped unconsciously. He was just fucking around with 2-Tall how he always did and got caught up in the moment when he threw the remote, but it didn't hit 2-Tall on the shoulder like he expected, it slapped Malina on the side of her face.

Malina felt the blow to the face but couldn't believe it. She turned around and stared at Dinero with the same shocked expression he had molded onto his face. Barbaric thoughts of retaliation plagued her mind. She once had a pair of men's eyes poked out just for staring at her impolitely, but as she looked down at, Dinero she just couldn't do it.

"You are *soooo* lucky I like you boy! Like, *very* lucky! Don't let that happen again. I know how y'all play, but when I'm around, cut it out because I'm not the one for games or second chances, so count this warning as a blessing," she warned intensely making sure to get her point across.

Dinero, 2-Tall, and Ladie all released the breath they were holding. Nobody knew how Malina's psychotic ass would react to the offense, even if it was a mistake.

"I'm so sorry, sis! You know it wasn't meant for you, but like you said, I'll stop playing," Dinero promised genuinely.

A pair of hands started clapping slowly in the distance. All four of them looked at the hallway, and the man that emerged around the corner took all of them for a loop. His face was very familiar. It was the same face on Ronte's latest mixtape cover called *Vonte*. His dreads were a little shorter now, but it was definitely Vonte in the flesh.

He walked toward them as he continued with the dramatic applause. He was dressed in black from head-to-toe with a pair of fitted cargo pants tucked inside a pair of high laced combat boots. A short-sleeved dry-fit shirt up under a lightweight bulletproof vest with plenty of deadly accessories attached to it.

By the look on everyone's face, Vonte could easily tell that everyone knew just who he was, and that's exactly how he wanted it. "I done did my homework on you Malina and it's not like you to spare a nigga, or bitch. I really can't say too much about it though because I done spared a muthafucka before, nobody's perfect."

"What? How the fuck did you get in here?" Malina asked with traces of Latino in her accent that got thicker as her anger rose, and she was literally struggling to keep her cool at this point.

Vonte smiled showing his sparkly gold teeth. "You mean how I get past those three security details y'all had standing around? I'm not gon' lie they good, but not good enough."

"So, you mean to tell me that *you* killed all those trained guards singlehandedly?" 2-Tall asked in disbelief.

There had to be a secret tunnel in Dinero's mansion that nobody knew about because he had some of the best guards money could buy and Malina's guards were even better. There was no way a rookie like Vonte took out that many vets.

"I probably could've pulled it off single-handedly, but I got a small team, and we're very efficient," Vonte bragged truthfully. "To answer your question, your guards ain't dead. We just shot them all with tranquilized filled darts. They'll resurface in a few hours, or so."

Malina had the biggest pride in the room. She came from an entire family of untouchables. She was a fucking cartel princess, and Vonte was a peasant in her eyes. If he'd done his homework on her like he said, then he'd see this coming.

She came out of her purse that laid next to her on the loveseat with a small throwing blade and threw it at him with professional quickness. Vonte saw the blade flying toward his face in slow motion as he did a quick spin dodging it by an inch. When he came back around from his spin, Malina was already fumbling in her purse for another blade, but he had already drawn the silenced pistol from the holster on his hip and fired a round into her forehead before she could get her hand back out of the purse.

"Nooooo!" 2-Tall yelled as Malina flew out of his lap onto the floor.

Ladie started screaming as she hopped off the couch attempting to run out of the room, but Vonte fired a round into her back causing her to crash face-first onto the hardwood floor at the edge of the halfway entrance.

"Ahhhh!" Dinero was up on his feet charging at Vonte savagely, but Vonte jumped in the air doing a complicated flip over him right before impact causing Dinero to trip and fall onto the hardwood floor as well.

After landing on his feet, Vonte pointed his pistol at Dinero, but quickly caught himself and returned it to the holster. He respected Dinero too much to shoot him. "Y'all niggas chill, they not dead. I shot them with darts like everybody else. They'll be up in a few hours, but Malina might take longer to wake up since I shot her in the forehead, but she'll live."

"What the fuck is wrong with you, nigga?" 2-Tall asked as he stood up and faced Vonte. "You know what her uncle gon' do when he hears about this shit? Especially when he finds out it was one of my own that did it!"

Vonte shook his head. "Nope, not one of your own, I'm not DG anymore, remember?"

"I know who you are, I know what you did, and I know what you about. What I don't know is your purpose, right now? What you gain by coming in here and showing your ass, other than a bigger price tag on your head?" asked 2-Tall curiously.

Vonte walked to the sofa that Ladie was on and helped himself to a seat. "No, I'm not gon' get a bigger price tag on my head, but the complete opposite. I could've easily killed your security. What that tell you? I'm not the rookie I once was. I'm a professional mercenary now."

Dinero looked at Vonte in disgust. "Shawty, you could've just pulled up on us if you wanted to talk. You ain't have to do all this shit!"

"With all due respect, Dinero, yes the fuck I did. I wanted y'all to see how easy it was for me to take down the people y'all looked to for protection," said Vonte.

"Tell us exactly what you want, so we can be done with this," 2-Tall commanded irritably. Never in a million years did he ever think Vonte would resurface like this.

"Like I said, I just wanted y'all to see how easy it'll be for me to disassemble your security."

Dinero looked at 2-Tall, and back at Vonte who was standing up. "That's it, that's all?"

"Yup, I'll be in touch though. I have a lot of work ahead of me, but just know this won't be your last time seeing me," Vonte informed before disappearing down the hall.

CHAPTER 28

When the government hired special agent Chinx to lead the investigation on Dilluminati in Georgia they did it because he was never known to play fair. He was known to do whatever it took to eliminate his targets from the game, he became possessed with each investigation, and agent Gill was learning that firsthand.

They were in a small abandoned lot on the Westside of Atlanta. Gill was told to meet him there to give him a report on what she'd learned since her last report.

"It's been three and a half months, Gill! You mean to tell me we don't have *anything* solid on them yet? I put you in the field because you convinced me, and everybody else in this operation that you could get results," Chinx scolded sternly. He was deeply considering pulling her out of the field.

"I mean we have cases on a few foot soldiers, but it's going to take time for the made-men. They've been moving smarter lately, way more strategic," she informed.

Chinx scratched the red stubble that was growing on his face as he stared up at her steadily. "Why do you think that is?"

"Well—I recently noticed they'd started making the transition ever since Dinero got out. Maybe that has something to do with it." She didn't know if Chinx's question was sarcastic or not but she gave her honest opinion anyway.

Chinx nodded. "I'll take that, but that doesn't stop the fact that we need results woman. I skipped over several more qualified agents to give you a shot but you're making me regret my decision," he admitted bluntly. "What about LaKisha, nothing?"

Gill shook her head reluctantly. "I'm afraid not. Mazi lost interest in her and it would look too suspicious for her to try to jump in the game herself, so she's basically useless."

Chinx gave her a knowing look. "That's ironic because that's exactly how I'm beginning to feel about you as well."

"I'm afraid I have some more bad news for you," she informed.

"You're kidding me, right?"

Gill shook her head *no*. "I might as well lay it out now. Purp lost interest in me about three weeks ago. He won't answer my texts or calls. It's like I never even existed to him."

"Wowwww!" Chinx shouted in disbelief. "And when were you planning on telling me about this?"

"I just didn't want you panicking like you're doing now. I miscalculated. I know he's a ladies man, but I felt that if he got a taste of a real good girl he'd keep her around, but I was obviously wrong."

Chinx laughed in her face. "Sounds like your feelings are hurt. I told you that avenue was pointless, he's a womanizer. That's what he does even to pretty, good girls like yourself. Hump you, then dump you. I expected that from the start, but I also expected you to get *some* kind of information out of him between that time. I'm sorry, Gill. I'm going to have to pull you out," he informed before hopping in his BMW coupe and pulling off slowly.

Gill wanted to cry, she'd blown her chance at elevating her career to the next level. She'd sacrificed her dignity and went against her life-long morals for her dream, now they were crushed. She was crushed, and could no longer hold the tears back, so she cried.

Little did she know, she'd be doing a lot more of that in the future. Purp left her a little surprise.

***

Monster walked through South DeKalb Mall with ZyAsia and a few Mobsters on his kill team. ZyAsia wanted them to buy some matching shoes for an upcoming photoshoot that they had scheduled. Her belly was now showing, and she wanted to get some good pregnant pictures with her baby's father. It was the beginning of September and fall was right around the corner, but it was still the very end of summer, and very hot, so plenty of people were out enjoying the summer weather.

ZyAsia had a pleasant expression on her face, but Monster's opposed hers. "Why the hell you wait until the mall is crowded, then you want to come?" he asked irritably while watching the crowd.

She knew how paranoid he was, but she insisted on taking a midday trip to the mall, and he wasn't going to let her go by herself, so there he was.

She looked over at him expectantly with a slight shrug of her shoulders and a few bobs of the head. "Who the hell wants to be in an empty mall? You always taking the fun out of shit. Damn! Just pretend to be regular for one day."

"When we first started talking, you said you chose me because I *wasn't* a regular nigga. Now you confusing me. What you want, woman?" he asked mockingly with a raised eyebrow.

"You get on my nerves!" she said with a roll of the eyes.

"I always get on yo' nerves when I'm speaking some real shit, but we ain't gon' talk about that though," he countered sarcastically.

She cringed at his cockiness. "Let's go get these shoes before we end up fighting in these folks mall."

Monster was about to hit her back with some slick shit until the Mobster in front of them stopped dead in his track's like a dog who'd just heard a strange noise in the distance. Monster looked past the mobster into the cold eyes of a killer. His protective instincts immediately kicked in, he quickly grabbed ZyAsia's arm and spun her around.

"Take her to the food court and don't take y'all eyes off her!" he instructed the two Mobsters that was walking behind them.

ZyAsia could hear the urgency in his voice, and knew better to resist, so she just went with the mobsters to the food court like she was told.

Monster turned back around and walked up to the last Mobster that was with him. He was still locked in on the threat when Monster walked up next to him. "These niggas crazy, but not stupid. If they approaching us in a public place, it's a chance they don't want smoke, but be on point just in case."

The Mobster nodded his head without taking his eyes off the oncoming group of shooters.

"Why you so tense, big boy? You know I'm smart enough not to pull a move in a mall," Killa stated as he closed in on Monster.

"I know you are but not them," Monster said referring to the eight shooters he had trailing him closely.

Killa motioned toward the Mobster next to Monster. "Shit, your boy don't look like he got all his screws his damn self."

"He missing enough to handle the business whenever, and where ever. What's the problem? You got something you need to tell me?" Monster asked defensively with his chest poked out.

Killa smirked devilishly keeping eye contact with the beast in front of him. "I really like y'all Dilluminati niggas. Even against the odds, y'all niggas gon' stand up in that paint. I can respect it, but that respect don't mean shit when y'all coming in between my money."

"I can't remember taking nothing from y'all niggas. So, what you talking about?" Monster asked curiously.

"A nigga ain't took shit around this way. Like I said, I like y'all niggas, so I'm gon' leave you wit' this lil' bit of advice. Kick that nigga Spider to the curb because he gon' get y'all fucked up."

CHAPTER 29

After the incident at Dinero's house last night, 2-Tall wanted to go back to the residence he shared with Malina a few hours away, but that wasn't possible. All the guards were fast asleep. The only people, other than himself, who weren't drugged was Dinero and his son Dee Gee.

Using Dinero's help, he dragged all the guards into the house. By the time they were finished the team of emergency private doctors, he called up had arrived. They immediately set up all their equipment and went to work making sure everyone's vitals were steady and whatnot.

Just like Vonte predicted Malina slept longer than everyone else. She didn't wake until the next evening, and 2-Tall was right there in the bedroom with her when she opened her eyes.

She came into consciousness slowly fighting off the powerful drug with plenty of effort. 2-Tall got up out of the chair he sat in, grabbed the glass on water off the nightstand, and put it to her lips for her.

"Drink this, baby. You need it," he assured while holding her head up, so she could sip from the cup properly.

She drunk half the cup, then pushed it away. She still felt weak and dazed, but she was fine. That is until her memory from the night before started kicking in. She laid her head back own on the pillow and started evaluating the entire situation.

"How you feeling, baby? You alright?" 2-Tall asked with much concern.

"Leave me alone. I'll figure out what to do with you by the time this shit wears off me," she said in a low voice.

2-Tall began to protest but thought better of it. He was hoping Malina would wake up with short-term memory loss, but that would've been too good to be true. He was responsible for Dilluminati, and Vonte still represented that brand as long as he was breathing, so 2-Tall would have to pay for what he did.

He bent down and tried to kiss her but she moved her face. "Get out! All this is your fault," she spat angrily.

2-Tall wanted to plead his case so badly, but it was no point. Malina was the opposite of understanding, so he just left the room with a lot on his mind, wondering what would become of the two of them.

***

Alexis was a beautiful chocolate woman of twenty-five years. Her thickness was a gift from God, but she worshipped herself like she was the one that made the creation. When her mother died ten years ago, her big sister Sapphire spoiled her rotten and gave her the game. The problem with her being spoiled most of her life, is that it made her very lazy, dependant, and expectant. So, when Sapphire started getting on her about earning her own money, she did the only logical thing that made sense to her. She searched for someone else to spoil her, and Toe-Tag just so happened to be the nigga she chose to do it.

She'd been following him on Instagram for a while, and he hadn't followed her back until AK said something about her. After that, they were messaging each other constantly, but Toe-Tag was so busy that it took a few weeks for him to squeeze some time in for her.

He pulled up in front of her house she shared with her sister in Atlantic Station. There was a black AMG Benz truck, and an Escalade sitting in front of her house. Toe-Tag texted her telling her to come outside.

"I don't know, girl. You might have to go by your damn self," her best friend Iyani informed nervously while looking out the window.

Alexis was putting the finishing touches on her make-up and looked at Iyani through the mirror. "Just last night you was all amped up about this. Now you want to back out? You lame for that one."

"Man, I was talking to my cousin last night about Toe-Tag. He told me to be careful because them niggas crazy. If my crazy ass cousin telling me about how crazy other niggas is. I don't think I want nothing to do with them," Iyani reasoned.

Alexis turned around. "Girl, them niggas not going to do nothing to you. You really gon' leave me hanging?"

"You know you don't have to go, right?"

"I know, but I want to and you supposed to have my back," Alexis said before grabbing her bag and leaving the house alone.

She walked down the driveway like a model on a runway knowing Toe-Tag and his crew had all eyes on her. Toe-Tag hopped out the back seat of the AMG to greet her, and her eyes lit up. He was even bigger, and sexier in person. Just how she liked them, and his reputation made her want him even more.

"You lookin' good, shawty," he complimented scanning her like a male lion does its prey. "You did that on purpose?"

She looked down at the cute black miniskirt she wore with the Chanel heels to match. "Yup, I know all y'all wear is black, so I didn't want to be the only oddball."

"That's wassup. What happened to your friend?"

"She's sick."

He flashed a knowing smirk. "Alright, get in." He motioned towards the open car door.

"Sooo, where are we going?" asked Alexis once they got on the highway.

Toe-Tag dropped his phone on his lap and looked over at her. "Shit, you said you wanted to go out to eat."

"I'm not hungry anymore. You know how to bowl?" she asked.

"Bowl?" he asked with traces of amusement in his voice. "You hear this shit, Valencia?"

Valencia just shook her head with a smile while focusing on the road. "Yes, I hear it."

"Oh, I get it. You too gangster to bowl, huh?" Alexis asked with pursed lips.

"It's not even that, it's just—" Toe-Tag was saying before his business phone started ringing.

He held an index-finger up to her signaling her to hold on while he took the call. "Wassup?"

He listened to a short message while nodding his head in understanding before hanging up. His whole demeanor had changed. "I'm gon' have to take you back home, shawty."

"What? Oh, hell no! I just waited all this time to link up with you. I don't care what you going to do I'm coming with you," she stated seriously.

Toe-Tag sat there studying her carefully. Although he sensed seriousness, he could also sense fear. She was scared but determined to pursue what she wanted. He was a risk-taker, so he admired the act of bravery.

"It won't take long at all. I'll handle this, then we can hit the bowling alley before they close," he promised before instructing Valencia on where to go.

Alexis sat back in the smooth leather seat and took a deep breath. On top of her anxiety, she felt an overwhelming surge of excitement. Just being around a nigga like Toe-Tag made her feel so alive and rebellious. She didn't know about the next woman, but she always craved what she wasn't supposed to have.

CHAPTER 30

Kapo had recently given Toe-Tag dominion over a small warehouse on the outskirts of town. Every enforcer needed an isolated space on private property to torture his victims, and Kapo reluctantly agreed, so he finally found a spot for him about a month ago. This would be the first day that Toe-Tag got to break the place in. There were already a series of trucks outside the warehouse when they arrived.

"Look, Valencia gon' stay in the car with you while I go handle this business. I'm gon' leave two Mobsters out here to watch over y'all while I'm in there just in case," he told Alexis before quickly hopping out the truck and walking inside the warehouse with two mobsters.

"You got any tips for me to make it with this crazy man?" Alexis asked Valencia jokingly trying to make conversation.

Valencia turned around and looked Alexis in the eyes with intense seriousness. "*Run!*"

Toe-Tag took his shades off as he entered the warehouse. Mazi and Monster approached him as the two Mobsters that came in with Toe-Tag joined the semicircle with everyone else.

"You ain't have to come. We could've handled this easy," Mazi assured.

Toe-Tag shook his head. "Nah, I want to see this shit with my own eyes."

"Shit, me too. Ain't nothing like watching a nigga lose his virginity," Monster chimed in devilishly.

Toe-Tag and Mazi gave him the *eye* before walking off on his crazy ass.

Quavo stood there in the semi-circle with clenched teeth. He wanted to curse God for the situation he was in but he had nobody to blame but himself. If he would've never jumped in the game, his mother would've never done that stupid ass shit she did, and things wouldn't be the way they were now.

Toe-Tag was the type of nigga that liked to make a point and made one every chance he got. At first, Quavo was worried that his mother would come up missing, but Toe-Tag had other plans in mind. He figured he'd torture her instead of a quick death.

Toe-Tag cast LaKisha out of Georgia and out of Quavo's life. He made sure both parties understood they could never speak to, or see each other *ever* again. Toe-Tag peered into LaKisha's watery eyes and let her know that her son would be on the front-line for the rest of his days. The very thing she feared was now her reality. Quavo was officially a crash dummy.

Quavo looked down at a man who hung in the middle of the semi-circle they'd formed. He'd seen men hanging upside down from chains in the movies, but it was a totally different experience in real life. Especially since he knew he would be the one to take the man's life. Everybody in the warehouse had stolen a soul before, so he was trying to play it cool in the room full of killers, but it was hard. His heart rate accelerated as Toe-Tag walked forward with Mazi and Monster on his heels.

Toe-Tag came forward and untied the hood from the man's head. Spider looked around frantically trying to get a clear understanding of where he was. Mumbles escaped his mouth as he tried to talk through the duct tape covering it.

"I gave you a warning at the meeting, but you thought this shit was a game, huh? Look at you now," Toe-Tag said before painfully snatching the tape off Spider's mouth.

"It wasn't me! I told my guys what to do, and they started back serving G-Shine again. I had no idea they had upped the prices. I don't know which one of my Mafioso's was behind it, but I'm telling you, Toe-Tag! I promise you I told them what to do! I'll *never* put the camp at jeopardy!" Spider pleaded not bothering to hide the desperation in his voice.

"That's crazy! You know that's how Rampage ended up getting whacked?" Toe-Tag asked but didn't give him enough time to answer. "He never fucked up, somebody else in his camp fucked up a mission, but that's probably the biggest downside of being a made-man. You're literally responsible for everybody in your camp. I'm gon' let you in on a lil' secret. It was me who fucked up on that mission that got Rampage killed, and that's something I got to deal with for the rest of my life. I'm gon' let you in on another secret. Even though I would gladly die for my niggas, it's still one of my biggest fears to get whacked for another nigga's mistakes, but like I said, it comes with the title. When it's my time, I'm gon' take that shit like a G. I advise you to do the same," he said before placing the strip of duct tape back over Spider's mouth. He didn't want to hear another word from him, there was no need.

Toe-Tag's little speech hit Quavo hard. He was beginning to figure out how gritty and ruthless, the game really was. All he ever wanted was the glory and benefits that came from being in the game, but like every other naive kid eager to jump headfirst in the streets, he never considered the many downsides that came with it.

It was amazing how he masked his rising anxiety as everyone in the room stared at him. He wasn't worried about anybody else as he locked eyes with Toe-Tag. "This the part where you want me to shoot him?"

Monster stepped forward and placed a big machete in Quavo's hand.

"Nah, that's too easy. This the part where you take his head off," Toe-Tag informed smugly.

Spider's eyes popped wide open, and he began mumbling through the duct tape as he wiggled on the chain like a fish on a hook. He knew he would die in the warehouse, but what he didn't know was that the punishment was more so for Quavo than it was for him. He just fucked up at the wrong time because any other time, he would've received a quick, painless, death.

Quavo's adrenaline began to skyrocket, and it became impossible for him to hide. He had prepared himself to shoot Spider, not hack his head off. "You want me to take his head off his body?" he asked just to be clear, and also to buy himself a little time to pump himself up for the barbaric act.

Toe-Tag nodded his head at a steady pace. "Yeah, it's easy to shoot a nigga, but with that knife, it's another story. You get up close and personal. You feel the blood on yo' skin, the soul dripping from they body going into yours."

Toe-Tag motioned for Quavo to step forward, but Quavo was in a temporary coma just thinking about the task, so Monster gave him a slight push causing him to lurch forward a few steps almost falling onto his face.

He caught his footing and make his way to the middle of the semi-circle with Toe-Tag and an upside-down Spider. He looked down at Spider who was peering up at him with desperate eyes.

Toe-Tag lifted his head up from the chin. "I advise you to avoid eye contact on this one, though. You not ready for that life yet. Just stand behind him, grab his head with your left hand, and start swinging as hard as you can until his head falls off. You got to psych out lil' bro'. That's the only way you gon' get through this shit."

Tears fell down Quavo's face as he clenched his teeth and found something to think about that would take his mind away from the madness. He did as instructed and got behind Spider. They had to lower Spider down a little bit, so Quavo could carry out the job properly.

He grabbed a handful of Spider's nappy fro with his left hand and started hacking away savagely at Spider's neck. He released a savage roar with every swing, and just like Toe-Tag predicted, blood was *everywhere*, but he didn't stop. He thought about his mother as he continued. He put it in his mind that he had to go hard to keep her safe and started swinging even harder without any remorse, he was psyched out!

CHAPTER 31

After the little situation at the warehouse, Toe-Tag kept his promise and took Alexis to the bowling alley. She wanted to go to the one on the Southside called Metro Lanes. Metro Lanes was a very popular chill spot around the city, but Toe-Tag never had a reason to go until then. He sat on the bench inside the building putting his bowling shoes on while she sat next time him doing the same.

"Do they go with you everywhere?" Alexis asked referring to the Mobsters that shadowed him like the Secret Service does the President.

"Yeah, there's a lot of people that want me dead in this city," he informed truthfully. "That's a problem with you?"

She shook her head. "Nope, I like it. Makes me feel important and safe," she answered jokingly. "Just do me a favor whenever you with me."

"What's that?" he asked looking over at her.

"Whenever you're with me, try to forget about all your problems, and just try to enjoy yourself. That's what I'm here for."

Toe-Tag placed a diamond-covered hand on one of her thick thighs. "I'll try my best."

***

Monster walked into the downtown coffee lounge, found Jasmine, and took a seat next to her on the love seat.

"You're late as hell," she spat in a form of a greeting without looking up at him. She just typed away at an amazing speed on her iPad. She had a deadline to meet on an upcoming project.

"I had business to handle. I'm here, though. What's up?" he stated.

"You the one that said you needed to meet with me, Monster. I find it a little weird but I'm here. So, you tell me what's up," Jasmine said sassily.

"It's about Rinno," he informed suddenly.

She stopped typing and placed the iPad on her lap. "I hope you not here to tell me to stop fucking with him because that's not gon' happen, Monster. Every time a bitch gets something good—"

"Man shut upppp!" he interrupted. "Ain't nobody trying to make you stop fucking with the man, girl. We good with the Armenians, and we trying to keep it that way."

"Oh kayyyyyy. So, you still not telling me shit Monster."

"What I'm trying to tell you is that we need you to keep fucking with him. Y'all gon' be the glue behind our ties with them. You need to get pregnant by the nigga, too. The sooner you have kids with him, the better."

Jasmine looked at Monster's big ass like he was insane. "I got a pass, Monster. I'm an author, y'all don't got no right to be controlling my life like this."

He leaned in closer so she could hear him perfectly. "Jasmine, you smart enough to go along with this. You spent enough time around me, and especially Toe-Tag to know better than to go against this shit."

***

Later that night, Quavo stood in the shower washing the dried blood off his body. He was alone in the apartment that he once shared with his mother, but he felt alone all the way around the board. He was prohibited from contacting his mother in any kind of way, his grandmother had just passed not too long ago, his father didn't want anything to do with him, and his aunt was out of town in Texas, but he couldn't even talk to her because that's where his mother was forced to live. All he had was Dilluminati and they were a *very* dysfunctional family.

None of them cared that he'd taken his first life at the young age of twelve in the most gruesome way possible. He had nobody to comfort him, so he had no choice but to harden himself. He took so much for granted before his mother left, and now that adulthood was being forced upon him, all he wanted now was to be a kid again.

After he took Spider's head off, Toe-Tag left him with a few Mobsters that helped him chop Spider's body up so they could drop it into a barrel of acid. Quavo's whole world was fucked up. He didn't know how to feel about life anymore. He had nothing to look forward to but death.

Before Toe-Tag left, he looked Quavo in the eyes and told him to get used to it because there was a lot more to come for him. He would put in more work than everyone else and earn less. That was now the story of his life, and he still had a lot of life to live. Feeling completely drained, he just sat down in the shower and balled up while the warm water rained down on his body.

Malik D. Rice

CHAPTER 32

The next morning, Shanay left Lil' Tee with Jasmine while she picked up the rest of her things from Toe-Tag's condo. She would be moving into Jasmine's Lithonia apartment after Rinno got the new house ready for them. She would stay there until she figured out what she wanted to do. She just needed alone time like Jasmine had to find herself. It was a process that took time.

As she walked up the stairs of Toe-Tag's building, she prepared herself to be around him. She had to emerge herself in total self-control. Toe-Tag always sparked cords in her soul whenever she was in his presence, but she'd have to fight that feeling from now on because he was toxic and she knew she deserved way better for herself, and her son.

She rang the doorbell to the apartment and waited about a full minute before he answered the door. "It's eight o'clock in the morning, girl," he stated groggily wiping the cold from his eyes.

Shanay tried her best to keep eye contact with him because she could see that he only had on a pair of thin, grey, sweatpants from her peripheral vision. She had to stay strong because one look at that print in those pants, she'd be ready to drop to her knees, so she walked past him into the apartment.

He had packed all the extra clothes and shoes she left in a trash bag that leaned against the wall in the living area.

"Where's my antique lamps?" she asked with raised eyebrows. "I know you ain't think you was keeping those. I spent a whole day at an auction for those," she said while walking back to his bedroom where the lamps were.

"Shanay!" Toe-Tag called after her but she wouldn't stop.

Shanay walked into the room towards the nightstand on the side of the bed and began to unplug one but had to do a doubletake. There was a big bulge under the sheet on the bed. She stood straight up and looked down at the bed with a sideways look.

"Don't do it, Shanay," Toe-Tag urged from the doorway.

Shanay being the spiteful person she was snatched the sheet back revealing a thick, chocolate, woman who laid there completely naked.

Alexis opened her eyes and looked up at Shanay. At first, she was confused, then recognition set in, and a big smile appeared on her face. "You must be the baby mama?"

Shanay rolled her eyes at Alexis before turning around to face Toe-Tag. "Really, you knew I was coming, and you got this ugly-ass bitch in here?" She couldn't hide her anger if she wanted to.

"Ugly? Come on now, look at her. That's a real model bitch," he boasted confidently as he leaned on the doorpost.

Shanay turned back around and took a good look at Alexis. She couldn't even disagree the bitch was beautiful. She was basically a prettier, and thicker version of herself. Toe-Tag had literally upgraded, and it sent a blow to her ego but she kept it together.

Alexis laid there with a smug expression on her face feeling good about herself.

"You think shit funny now, huh? You ain't gon' be laughing for long, girl. This lifestyle is *not* sweet," Shanay warned seriously before collecting her belongings and getting up out of there as fast as possible.

Toe-Tag offered to help carry her things downstairs, but she declined. She didn't want him to see the tears that she finally released after stepping outside.

***

2-Tall called a meeting with the Billion Dollar Round Table. It consisted of all the Godfathers for Dilluminati throughout the country. Dinero wanted to show his face but 2-Tall strongly advised against it because he was too hot.

He rented a ballroom in downtown Manhattan for the occasion. The ballroom was huge, and he had it cleared out for the meeting. There was a long table in the middle of the room where they sat. A variety of foods were placed on the table for them to enjoy during the meeting.

2-Tall sat quietly at the head of the table as they feasted and chatted amongst themselves. He studied them closely and noticed that most of them were genuinely happy. He gave them purpose and belonging in life. Little did they know, they did the same for him. Just by him knowing that they depended on him, motivated him, and caused him to go harder.

"You aight, bro? You haven't said a word since we been here," Kapo said from the seat on the side of him.

"I'm about to now," 2-Tall informed before standing up to his full height looking down at everyone at the table.

He didn't have to clear his throat for them to quiet down, it came naturally. His superiority was well respected, and his words were always powerful, so they always listened.

"Hope everyone's enjoying the food and each other's company. I know rumor was out that Dinero was going to show his face at this meeting, but I'm afraid to inform everybody that he won't be able to show up at this meeting, or any other meeting we hold. He's a very public figure, and we can't afford the attention," he stated before taking his blazer off and tossing it on his chair.

He tucked the back of his Armani shirt in as he continued with the speech, "I rarely call big meetings like this to prevent attention, I would much rather pull up on y'all separately over time, but I have a very important announcement to make, and I don't want to repeat it thirty-six times. I don't want to repeat it at all, so listen closely. I'm going to start by letting y'all know it's officially over with for me, and Malina."

Some of the Godfathers just stared at 2-Tall open-mouthed, and some murmured with each other. All was expected from 2-Tall it was big bad news for them all.

"Y'all can rest easy because it's not over for our ties with the Mendez Cartel. We make them too much money, so that'll remain the same, but there will be changes in our agreement. Since I'm not with Malina anymore, we will no longer be getting the family discount from them. They're upping our prices." Some men let out exaggerated sighs, and some just shook their heads. This too was expected from 2-Tall. "I know, I know how y'all feeling, right now, but just believe me when I say, it could've been way worse. All y'all got to do is watch your spending habits and advise your camps to do the same. We still plugged in and that's all that counts. We just not getting spoiled anymore."

"What happened to you and Malina?" The Godfather for Louisiana asked the question everyone wanted to know.

2-Tall picked up the glass of champagne on the table in front of him and turned it up before putting it back down. "What you think, nigga? She caught me with another bitch," he lied with a straight face.

CHAPTER 33

Allo was Spider's top Mafioso and handled most of the business for Spider. They'd always been a team. Spider was the flashy one, while Allo was more low-key. People saw Spider more which is why Kapo chose him to be the Don when he got bumped up. Allo was genuinely happy for his friend, and happily took the spot as his right-hand man, but eventually, the position got to Spider's head. Made-men in Dilluminati were given so much praise that it boosted their ego which ate up all of their humbleness.

Spider fell victim to the made-man curse, and that's where he started to lose Allo as a friend. Spider's biggest mistake was treating Allo like he was inferior to him when in reality, Allo was basically the main reason Spider had made it that far.

The idea to cut ties with G-Shine originated from Allo who came up with most of the ideas for their camp anyway. It's been that way ever since Kapo left, so the fact that Spider refused to give him any credit, or recognition sparked a certain type of hatred inside him that he never knew he had.

Now that Spider was gone Allo didn't hate him so much, and actually regretted what had happened. When word got out about what happened to Spider, Allo cried for his friend. When he came up with the idea to up the prices on G-Shine he did so with the intention of getting Spider out of the way, but he never thought Spider would get whacked for something so petty. Maybe demoted or banned from the city but he never would've thought that Toe-Tag would've done Spider like that.

That was a week ago. Now, he was in the back of an Escalade on the way to participate in his first Don meeting. Papa summoned him to show up at KINKY at midnight. He dressed up in a nice Louis Vuitton ensemble and sported some of his best jewelry. When the Escalade parked outside of KINKY in the parking lot, he waited for one of the Mobsters to get out and open his door for him. He stepped out of the truck feeling like a new man. It was unfortunate what happened to Spider, and he wished it never went down like that, but it was already done, and there was no need to beat himself over it. He had to continue moving for himself, and the camp that he was now responsible for.

He entered the club through the back door and went inside the big VIP room while his kill team lingered around with the rest of the mobsters on the private floor. The other three Dons was already in the room waiting for Allo so they could get started. Allo found a seat on one of the sofas hoping that his tardiness wasn't offensive to them.

Papa was the only person in the room with a suit on and it fit him well. In his mind, he was a legitimate businessman, so he often dressed the part. He stood and faced the other three Don's in the room. "This isn't a formal meeting. We're here today because there's two new additions to this roundtable."

Papa went on explaining to them all the rules of the roundtable, and what was expected of them. He asked Toe-Tag if he had anything to say, he declined, so he asked the two new Dons the same.

Allo quickly declined the offer but Omega had something to say. He wasn't just Purp's younger cousin, he was Purp's living backup plan. Ever since Omega's age was in the double digits, Purp schooled him on the game. Omega wasn't as pretty as Purp but he wasn't ugly either. That with his flamboyant swagger, and smooth mouthpiece, he had what it took to pull a bad bitch wherever he went.

"This won't take too long. Everybody knows the situation with my cousin, and it affected a lot of people. After getting all the hoes tested in my camp, I'm down to fifteen right now, and they being overworked, right now. So, if y'all got some bad bitches y'all think would be good candidates, point me in their direction so I can reel 'em in. That's it," Omega said confidently. There was so much of Purp in him. He would do just fine in his cousin's shoes.

The meeting didn't even last a full five minutes, but it was definitely mandatory, so Papa had to call it. Papa was the first to leave because he had a flight to catch in a few hours. Omega was right after him, and Allo tried to leave with Omega, but Toe-Tag's voice stopped him at the door. "Aye, Allo! Come chop it up with a nigga real quick."

Allo turned around and faced Toe-Tag who was still seated comfortably on the sofa. "I got a meeting I'm late for," he informed shakily. He was shaky in Toe-Tag's presence and wanted to get out of the room with him as soon as possible.

"You're already late, a few more minutes won't hurt. Now close that door and sit back down. I think you gon' want to hear what I got to say," Toe-Tag said calmly, but firmly enough to indicate that Allo had no say-so in the matter.

Allo obliged, he didn't want to get on Toe-Tag's bad side because that didn't work too well for his predecessor. "What's up, bro?"

"Don't call me, bro. Looks to me, niggas that you consider to be your brother, you stab them in the back," Toe-Tag accused harshly.

Allo's face was a mask of confusion. "What?"

"Come on, man. Spider gave you the order to start back supplying the G-Shine's with the same prices, but you upped the prices knowing Spider would suffer consequences, but you just ain't know it was gon' be that severe. Nobody did." Allo just sat there quietly. "Don't even play wit' my intelligence by denying my accusations. I know what you did but it's all good, though. Everybody makes mistakes, but the things about those mistakes is they got to be paid for. For you, that's going to be literal. This the deal. In addition to the tax, you pay Pablo every month, you gon' kick the same amount of taxes to me."

"What? That's insane!" Allo informed seriously.

Toe-Tag shook his head in disagreement. "No, the agreement's not insane, I am. But you already know this, though which is why I think you'll pay. Like I said, mistakes have to be paid for. Just be lucky you're not paying with your life like Spider did." He got up and walked out of the room without another word or glance.

Once Toe-Tag was gone, Allo took a series of deep breaths to calm his spirit. "Karma's a muthafucka," he philosophized to himself.

CHAPTER 34

Mooski had been in DeKalb County Jail long enough to get comfortable. At first, he found it very difficult to adjust, but as the days went by, he got into the whole jail routine and it just got easier by the day.

He was in the seated area where inmates sat to watch TV. He sat with a few mobsters who were locked up for different reasons. They were watching a live episode of TMZ enjoying the few hours they had outside of their cells.

"Mario Parker! You have an attorney visit," the female guard informed through the intercom by the front door.

Mooski popped up with the speed of a squirrel and walked to the front door that was opened for him by the guard in the booth. The buildings in DeKalb's jail were two eight-story cylinders, so he had to literally walk around the hallway that wrapped around the watchtower to reach the stairs that lead to the visitation booths.

The guard popped the door to the third booth so Mooski could enter. Once he was inside, the door closed by itself locking him inside the booth. He took a seat on the stool facing the nicely dressed white man that sat on the other side of the thick glass waiting for him.

They picked up the phones at the same time in order to communicate. The lawyer spoke first, "Hi, Mr. Parker, I'm not going to ask how you're doing because I could only imagine, but I'm here to give you a little hope. I'm going to do everything in my power to build a good defense against the case the state has built against you."

Mooski was unfazed, he showed exactly no expression on his face as he stared the man in the eyes. "Fuck all that. I'm going to prison for the rest of my life no matter what you say in that courtroom. It is what it is. The only reason I came up here to meet with you is because Toe-Tag told me he needs to talk to me about some serious shit, and I know he sent a message through you. What is it?"

The lawyer knew from research that Mooski was a different type of individual. There was something in his eyes that he saw in Toe-Tag's as well. He didn't understand their kind at all, but they paid him well, so he'd do what they asked of him. He reached into his inner coat pocket, pulled out a piece of paper, and put it in the drop-box that was meant for legal papers. He closed the box and pushed it over to Mooski's side.

Mooski opened the box, grabbed the paper, unfolded it, and read the small typed letters. *Your boy Trouble done folded under the pressure. He talking to them folks. Find a way to handle that business. He was never Loyal 4Eva!*

Mooski ripped the paper up into tiny pieces while shaking his head disappointingly. He couldn't believe his childhood friend would go against the grain like that. Now he had to be the one to make sure Trouble got whacked. Shit didn't stop behind the walls, business still was handled in every way, just on a smaller scale.

***

Monster and Mazi had just finished running a good game of one-on-one basketball on the court in the park down the street from their hood. Since Mazi got out, Monster had been watching his diet and exercising.

They sat on one of the picnic tables watching a few of the mobsters run a two-on-two game. "You back fucking with that other girl now, huh?" Monster asked curiously.

Mazi was one of the most gangster niggas he knew, but he also was a lover boy, and Monster knew he couldn't go long without a girlfriend.

"I mean, we fucking. That'll never change, but I don't think I'll ever get back with her. She switched all the way up since I've been out of prison," said Mazi.

"You just need to focus on the money right about now anyway, bro. That and keeping Toe-Tag safe," Monster said as his phone started ringing. It was ZyAsia, so he got up and walked off to take the phone call.

Mazi put his T-shirt back on and watched the basketball game on the court. The four Mobsters on the court really seemed to be enjoying themselves, but Quavo just stood there like a zombie. To the average person, it would appear that he was watching the game, but Mazi knew better. His mind wasn't there in the park with them. He was zoned out.

"Aye, Quavo!" Mazi called out across the park.

Quavo looked up at Mazi who was signaling for him to come over there, so he made his way around there even though he didn't feel like talking to anyone.

"What's up, lil' nigga?" Mazi asked upon his arrival. Quavo remained quiet as he just shook his head for an answer. "What you got on your mind?" Another head shake from Quavo meaning *nothing*. "Come here and take a seat. I got something for you." Quavo complied. "You ain't been talking much since your mother left, and even less after that day in the warehouse. You showed everybody you got the savage in you, but at the end of the day you still only twelve. So, I know it's fucking with you," Mazi said before digging into his Nike gym bag.

He came out with a small hand-sized Bible. He took Quavo's hand and placed it inside his palm. "I know you probably think God don't want nothing to do with niggas like us, but that's wrong thinking. Get to reading. He's a God that's all about forgiveness."

Quavo looked down at the book, and back up at Mazi. "You really think this will help?"

"It got me through my roughest times, so I'm giving it to you during yours. Take out your phone and look up the word *repent*."

CHAPTER 35

Freddy had been healing tremendously, but he still followed the doctor's orders by taking it easy. He hadn't left his house in Dunwoody since he'd been released from the hospital, so Masio took it upon himself to hold their traditional dinner meetings at Freddy's house until he was well enough to start going out again.

They had a professional soul food catering service to cook and serve them their food. "These ribs on point, too! We need to order from this same company next time," Freddy advised.

Masio gave him a knowing look. "Shouldn't be no next time, bro. You need to get your ass out of this house. You can't stay in here forever."

"Why I can't? Kapo told me to make sure business stays handled, he never said from where," Freddy reasoned.

Their conversation was interrupted by a third party's presence. Vonte walked into the dining room casually and took a seat at the table. He didn't even say anything, just sat right there typing something on his phone like everything was gravy.

Freddy and Masio exchanged surprised looks before settling their eyes back on Vonte who was dressed in the usual tactical gear he kept on these days.

"Vonte! What the fuck you doing here, nephew?" Freddy asked with wide eyes. "Why you ain't let me know you was coming?"

Vonte smiled at his uncle. "I'm here to check on you fool. What else? And you need to get used to me popping up like this because that's how I'm coming from now on."

"What's up, man? I missed you, nephew. How you been doing?" Freddy wanted to ask where he'd been but knew better.

"I been real busy lately, handling business that needs handling. You'll hear about it," Vonte assured.

Freddy smiled, he was beyond happy to be in the presence of his favorite nephew again. "You popped up on your brother like this?"

"Nah, I'm gon' pull up on him next," Vonte said now eating from Freddy's plate.

"I got a question for you, lil' bro," Masio said eyeing the young killer.

Vonte motioned for him to get on with it.

"What you gon' do now?"

"I'm making up plans as I go," Vonte answered honestly.

***

Toe-Tag, Mazi, and Monster were at AK's condo catching up with him making sure he was alright. AK was one of the many made-men who decided they were safer in the house, so Toe-Tag went out of his way to check on his friend.

"I saw that picture Alexis posted of y'all together. You done put the round-house-special on that girl already?" AK asked jokingly making everyone in the room laugh including himself.

"Hell no, nigga. I ain't just going around hitting hoes with that shit. I don't know how she fucked up over a nigga like that. I just hit her with the lazy dick. She was riding me the whole time," Toe-Tag retorted honestly.

Monster started laughing so hard he almost fell off the chair he sat in. "Aye! Tell him about Shanay, though."

AK looked at Toe-Tag with wide eyes. "Noooo! She popped up? You a dirty nigga, boy."

"Man, that's on the Fours I forgot I told Shanay to come get her shit that morning. She wasn't even about to go in the room until she thought about them lamps. She was *hot* shawty!" Toe-Tag informed enthusiastically drawing them all into the story. He'd always been a good storyteller. "She saw Alexis in the bed and had the nerve to try and call the bitch ugly."

"Alexis is a lot of things but she far from ugly," AK admitted. He was talking more, but his voice hadn't improved any.

Toe-Tag nodded in agreement. "That's what I told her, and she couldn't even argue with it. She just threw salt on my name to Alexis, grabbed her shit, and left. I think she cried in the car, too."

"My lil' nigga the G.O.A.T out here," Mazi said proudly while putting a hand around Toe-Tag's shoulder proudly.

"Nahhhhhh! I got to disagree on that one. Last time I checked I was the G.O.A.T out here," Vonte said as he walked through the front door with Facts and Millie behind him.

Toe-Tag, Mazi, Monster, and AK upped their guns to train them on Vonte, but Facts and Millie was way faster. They shot Monster, Mazi, and AK before they even got their fingers on their triggers.

"Just tranquilizer bullets, they'll be back up sooner-than-later," Vonte informed before pushing Monster off his chair onto the ground and taking a seat himself. "Put the gun down, so we can talk."

"Fuck you, shawty!" Toe-Tag spat intensely. He wanted to whack Vonte so bad. All he saw was Rampage's dead face looking up at him that cold night.

Vonte pulled his phone out, tapped it a few times, placed it on the wood floor, and slid it over to Toe-Tag. "Take a look at that there."

Toe-Tag picked the phone up out of curiosity and dropped it just as fast. It was a picture of Shanay and Lil' Tee in a checkout line at a grocery store. He was clenching his teeth so hard it was beginning to hurt.

"Don't worry. They're still alive. I just wanted you to know that I know where they at. I don't care where you move them, or how many times. I promise you, I'll find them. You outsmarted me last time, and that was your last time," Vonte informed seriously.

"If you gon' whack me, go ahead and get it over with," Toe-Tag instructed fearlessly.

Vonte waved him off. "You know if I wanted you dead, you'd be in hell already. Pick the phone back up and look at the rest of the pictures."

Toe-Tag did as he was told. The next few pictures were pictures of bodies that were lined up on the ground. It was Dead Shot and his kill team. At first, he thought they were just sleep from tranquilized bullets like his guys, but the blood told otherwise. They were all dead.

"They had to go, and you know why. Facts and Millie wanted to roll with me, but I didn't let them. I took all them niggas down singlehandedly. It was real personal," Vonte informed after Toe-

Tag slid the phone back across the floor. "At first, you was on that list, but for *some reason,* my ancestors don't want me to whack you. You already marked for death, so they just want me to let the universe handle you."

Toe-Tag chuckled amusingly. Vonte was on some more shit these days. "Your ancestors got me fucked up. But anyway, if you not here to kill me, what you here for?"

"Just to let you know that I could've touched you. To let you know that you won a battle back then, not the war. It's levels to this shit, lil' nigga. Oh yeah, don't let this meeting get back to Kapo. My ancestors want me to leave him alone. I've caused him enough pain," Vonte informed matter-of-factly before leaving the condo the way he came with his minions on his heels.

CHAPTER 36

2-Tall was abruptly torn out of a deep sleep as a weight was added onto his body causing him to sink deeper into the soft mattress.

"I should cut your fucking throat," A familiar voice growled with a large sharp blade pressed on his windpipe.

2-Tall opened his eyes to the sight of Malina's crazy ass. She'd been on top of him like this plenty of times in the middle of the night, but never with the knife. He tried to push her off him, but she pressed her weight down harder causing the blade to draw a droplet of blood from his skin.

"How you get in here?" He asked.

"I'm the one that bought you this house. You think I don't have a key?" she said. "I really want to cut your throat, but my uncle won't let me. He says you're too valuable but I'm the one that made your black ass!"

"Kill me for what? What another nigga did?" he asked confusingly. She was probably the hardest person on earth to understand.

"I want to kill you for not killing him but it doesn't matter because you're protected by my uncle. Looks like you finally got what you wanted," she informed knowingly.

"Once again, wasn't nobody trying to use you, Malina," he assured.

She pressed the knife even deeper into his neck so he wouldn't be able to talk any further. "Shut up! You were in love with your baby mother this whole time. Don't play with my intelligence. It's alright, though. The dick was good while it lasted. I'll buy me another man in no time. I just hope this one knows how to love me correctly. Anyway, this isn't meant to be a long visit. I just came to let you know I'm going back to Mexico. The DEA is on my trail, so my uncle is pulling me out, but my little cousin's stepping up, and he makes me look like a saint. You're on thin ice, baby boy," she informed wickedly before hopping off him and swaying out the room with her usual nonchalant prance.

***

Babie had just returned to the hood from visiting Mooski at the county jail. It was hard for her to see him in there like that, but at least he seemed to be coping with the situation. He told her not to wait on him and to move on with her life. She didn't lie to him like most other females did to their incarcerated men. She let him know that she was still young, and would move on with her life, but assured him that she would never forget about him and would always be there for him. He seemed content with that when she departed from him.

A few Mobsters from the hood escorted her to the jail since she didn't have her license. After the visit, she told them to take her to Kamya's spot. It had been a minute since she saw her big sister and felt like this was the best time to visit.

She didn't care too much for Handsome but he treated Kamya right, so she dealt with him. He answered their door like always with his AK-74 in hand looking all paranoid. "Boy, do you ever leave the damn house? All up under my sister and shit. Let the bitch breathe!"

Handsome stared at Babie sideways as she brushed past him like a mini hurricane. If he didn't respect Kamya so much, he probably would've slapped the taste out of her mouth. "I don't see her complaining," he retorted after closing the door behind her.

Kamya was on the couch rubbing her big belly looking up at them through squinted eyes. "I wish y'all stop fighting. Why can't y'all just get along?" she asked desperately.

"Okay, I'll leave yo' boo alone," Babie promised taking a seat on the sofa next to her sister.

Handsome blew Kamya a seductive kiss and flashed Babie a malicious glance before going back into his office. He had a lot of work to do.

"You never happy for me. You, Rampage, or mommy! Why y'all can't never let me be happy?" Kamya asked seriously while eating from a tub of pecan ice cream.

Babie poked her lip out and batted her eyes innocently. "I'm sowwy sisterrrrr! I was just messing with him. I'm definitely happy for you and hope everything works out. I love you, girl. You all I got left."

"I love you too, Babieeeee!" Kamya responded emotionally. Her pregnancy had her more sentimental than usual.

Kamya placed the container of ice cream on the table so Babie could lay down on her lap like she always did.

"I just came from seeing Mooski at the jail," Babie informed sadly.

Kamya rolled her eyes. "I mean, it's sad but even I saw that coming. Why you acting like it's a surprise, Babie?"

"I knew it was coming but damn—I don't know, I guess it was just too soon," Babie responded.

"How he doing in there? He going crazy I bet," Kamya predicted.

Babie shook her head in disagreement. "Nope, it's crazy because it's like the opposite with him. Most niggas do lose they minds when they get locked up, especially with all that damn time he's facing, but it really seems like Mooski's finding his mind in there. That just might've been the best thing to happen to him."

Malik D. Rice

CHAPTER 37

Shanay had shit to do so she dropped Lil' Tee off on Toe-Tag who didn't mind at all because he loved spending time with his seed. He sat on the floor in Lil Tee's room watching him play with a pile of Lego blocks. The little nigga was looking like him more and more as the days passed. Of course, he wanted a better life for his son but it was seeming impossible. As long as Vonte was alive his entire family's life was in danger and that didn't sit right with him period. He racked his brain trying to come up with a magical plan to defeat Vonte for good. The world obviously wasn't big enough for the two of them.

"Damn, shawty!" he spat in frustration as he laid down on his back with his eyes closed.

Lil' Tee sensed that his father was bothered and immediately stopped what he was doing to comfort him. "Daddy! You ooo-kay?" he asked in his little angelic voice.

That voice seemed to give Toe-Tag the strength he needed to open his eyes and put a big smile on his face. "Yeah, I'm good, lil' nigga! Come here!" He picked Lil' Tee up and started bench pressing him into the air while making strange noises that caused Lil' Tee to laugh joyfully. They needed each other.

A few hours later, Lil' Tee was knocked out in his rocket ship bed and Toe-Tag was still up trying to ensure a safer future for his family when Dreek texted his phone claiming they needed to meet as soon as possible. There was no way Toe-Tag was about to leave his son in the house alone, so he told Dreek to come to his spot.

It took Dreek an hour to show up because he was still on the road when he contacted Toe-Tag, but he showed up like always. He knocked on the door instead of ringing the doorbell like Toe-Tag instructed.

"Wassup, bro'? Tell me something good," Toe-Tag said after letting Dreek in and returning to his seat at the dining room table.

Dreek walked in and sat across from him. "I'm not gon' lie man, it's all bad."

"Come on, Dreek! Don't tell me that, shawty. I told you not to fuck this one up. That's why I sent Monster with you," Toe-Tag stated heated.

At the mention of Monster's name, Dreek averted eye contact by dropping his head down to the table and shaking it.

"What?" Toe-Tag asked in exaggeration. "Dreek! You better tell me what the fuck happened!" he spat after banging both fists on the table causing the dishes and Dreek, to jump where they sat.

"Shit went left, bro'! We went to Killa's spot, the one you gave us the address to, and he was there like you said. We kicked the door down asking him where the drugs was but he just started laughing. So, Monster tied him up and started beating on the nigga while I watched Killa's bitch making sure she didn't do nothing crazy."

"What was the other two Mobsters doing while y'all was doing that?" Toe-Tag cut him off from the story.

"They was tearing the house up looking for the drugs, or anything else they could find," Dreek answered shortly just in case Toe-Tag had more questions.

Toe-Tag motioned for him to continue to the story.

"So, while this nigga Monster was beating on Killa he just kept laughing, telling us that we might as well kill him because his shooters was gon' hunt us down. As soon as the Mobsters got back in the bedroom with the drugs and money they found, we heard a bunch of car doors closing. I ran to the window and saw at least twenty niggas hop out of trucks and make their way in the house. Monster whacked Killa and his bitch off the top, then told us to get ready. The plan was to fight them off as long as we could before they ended up whacking us. We all knew we was dead."

Toe-Tag motioned for him to stop. "So, you telling me Monster's dead?"

The pain and raw emotion in Toe-Tag's voice hit Dreek *hard*. "Yeah, man, I'm sorry! He didn't make it. Him or the other two Mobsters."

"So, how is it that I'm sitting here talking to yo' ass without a muthafuckin' scratch on yo' body?" Toe-Tag barked savagely with tears in his eyes.

The disgusting look Toe-Tag was giving Dreek made him feel like less than nothing. "I ran to the shower and hid in the tub. I thought they would've come and found me, but they never did. They whacked Monster and the Mobsters, then got the fuck up out of there when they heard the police sirens. Once I was sure they was gone I got up out of there too right before the police came. It wasn't nothing else I could've done bro'! I'm sorry man!"

Toe-Tag couldn't hold it in anymore. He stood up and flipped the table over in the same motion causing all the dishes to crash onto the floor. Dreek jumped back in his chair out of fear and crashed just as hard as the dishes.

Toe-Tag was on top of him within a matter of seconds. "You a *bitch*! You a *hoe*! You a *fuck nigga*! You was supposed to stand beside him and die with him, nigga! You don't deserve to be alive, right now. But I'm not gon' kill you because I need you," he informed truthfully before letting go of Dreek's shirt and going to check on his crying son.

About two hours later, Dreek opened the door for Shanay. Toe-Tag had called her to come pick Lil' Tee up early. He never told her why, but she could hear the distress in his voice, so she came without question.

"Where they at?" she asked Dreek who looked like shit but she didn't acknowledge the fact.

"They in the bathroom," he informed with a raspy voice like he was crying and returned to his seat on his chair.

Shanay took notice of the big mess in the dining room and started speed walking towards the bathroom. Something was very wrong, and she was beginning to worry. She'd never seen Dreek look so miserable in her life.

She walked into the bathroom with intentions on demanding to know what was going on, but the sight she witnessed upon opening the bathroom door stopped her dead in her tracks and brought instant tears to her eyes.

Toe-Tag was taking a bath with Lil' Tee. He sat in the tub balled up with his head in his knees and arms while Lil' Tee stood up hugging his father as tight as he could. Toe-Tag was sobbing and Lil' Tee was doing the same.

Shanay's tears started flowing heavier as she rushed over to the tub, dropped on her knees, and hugged both of them. There was nothing to say, she just wanted to be there for her baby's father. He needed someone and she vowed to always be there for him even if they weren't in an actual relationship. They would always be family.

CHAPTER 38

When Allo heard about the incident that happened at Killa's house, he smiled inwardly while faking concern in front of his Mobsters. Toe-Tag fucked up when he decided to make Allo an enemy instead of a friend. After the meeting at KINKY, Allo went on a short fishing trip the next day. Being surrounded by the water cleared his mind and he came up with his best thoughts while fishing.

He evaluated the situation but more importantly, he evaluated his opponent. He was aware of the fact, Toe-Tag was no dummy. He was very smart for a man of his age, but he often let his muscle overshadow his brain. Since muscle was respected, and brainpower was usually underestimated, his pride naturally led him to use his muscle most of the time, and Allo took advantage of that.

After that little fishing trip, he requested a sit-down with Toe-Tag. He showed up with $20,000 and gave it to Toe-Tag once he showed up at the pool hall. Toe-Tag asked what the money was for, Allo let him know that there was a job that needed to be done. He lied by saying he fronted the G-Shines some drugs that they never paid for and wanted Killa's head for it.

Toe-Tag instinctively gave the money back and informed Allo that the job couldn't be done. Allo anticipated he'd do that, so he planned ahead. *"You might as well take the job. I obviously came to you for a reason. You're the best at what you do. All you have to do is not get caught and G-shine will never know what hit them. If you don't think you can handle it, I'll probably just take the complaint to Pablo who's just gon' go to Freddy who will probably make you do it for free, after he convinces Kapo of course."*

Allo could literally see Toe-Tag's pride eating away his good sense. He said *fuck it* and snatched the money out of Allo's hand assuring that the job would get done. Then he went on telling Allo what would happen if he ever talked about this meeting before ended the meeting by walking out of the pool hall with his kill team in tow.

As Allo stood there watching Toe-Tag leave, he felt a surge of triumph run through his body. He knew all about Killa's track record as well and calculated that he'd at least leave one of Toe-Tag's Mobster's dead on the scene giving solid evidence of Toe-Tag's deceit, therefore, sparking a war that would end up falling on Toe-Tag.

Being the supreme thinker that he was Allo decided to tip one of the G-Shine's off about the hit on Killa at the last minute, giving them just enough time to catch Toe-Tag's Mobsters at the house. The plan was solid. Allo couldn't help but think how far he would've made it in the game if he'd been playing dirty the whole time. Seems like you had to play dirty to get anywhere in the game that they played.

***

"Nooooo! Whyyy? You took my baby from me!" ZyAsia accused hysterically as she sobbed on the bedroom floor of her apartment while rubbing her huge belly. "It's all your fucking faulttt!"

Toe-Tag stood over her with tears pouring down his face. After Shanay left, he got dressed and walked straight to her apartment to break the news to her. It was one o'clock in the morning when he showed up on her doorstep, and she was up waiting on Monster to return as usual. When she opened the door and saw Toe-Tag and Dreek standing at the door with devastated looks, she ran to the room shouting at the top on her lungs. She knew what it was.

Dreek tried to help her up off the floor but she kicked him in the dick making him double over in pain instantly. "Aggggghhh fuckkk!"

"Get the fuck outttt! I hate y'all! My baby got to grow up without a father! Get outttt!" she bellowed so hard that she frightened Toe-Tag a little and that was saying a lot.

Toe-Tag helped Dreek back up onto his feet and dragged him up out of there. There was nothing they could do for ZyAsia at the moment, she had to mourn her loss by herself.

***

"Man, I woke up to this bitch on top of me with a big sharp ass knife to my throat," 2-Tall told Kapo as they watched the ocean water crash against itself from Kapo's balcony in his San Francisco home.

Kapo couldn't help but laugh at his friend. "That's crazy. Shit, you need to be grateful she ain't chop yo' dick off, nigga," he informed seriously. It was no secret to Malina's mental state.

"Yeah, I guess you right," said 2-Tall.

Kapo had quickly become one of 2-Tall's closest confidants over the months. 2-Tall wanted to tell Kapo the real reason behind his breakup with Malina, but that would require him to tell him about Vonte, and he really didn't want to do that. It wouldn't do anything but cause Kapo more pain. Especially since Vonte was virtually unstoppable. He was like a lethal ghost. You never knew when he was coming, or when he'd strike. So, there was really no reason to rip the bandage off Kapo's healing wounds. He would give Vonte what he wanted and continue to run Dilluminati accordingly. Nobody had to know about his secret assassins.

CHAPTER 39

Boc! Boc! Boc! Boc! Boc!

Quavo shot back at a Jeep truck full of G-Shine shooters who chased after him on his four-wheeler. He called himself pulling a Rampage move, by riding into enemy territory to drop some opposition. He succeeded with the first part of the mission, by pulling up into Victory Crossing Apartments and shooting at a group of G-Shine soldiers who stood on the corner, but the second part was the hardest. He couldn't seem to get away. It's like they had shooters on standby for an oncoming assault.

As Quavo stuck the pistol back into his waistband and grabbed the handles with both hands so he could steer the ATV properly, he thought about his short life and came to the quick conclusion that he hadn't lived enough of it.

The shooters in the truck behind him were on his ass. They were determined to end his young life. There was a war going on in the streets, and he took it upon himself to hop in the field solo, now he was suffering the consequences. He hit a hard, right turn that brought the ATV onto two wheels for a second, but luckily, he didn't flip it over. When the other two wheels hit the ground, he hit the gas and took off as the big Ford Fusion struggled to make a quick sharp turn.

Quavo maneuvered through the backstreets expertly trying to make it to Candler Road where he'd be able to lose them. A group of kids were playing basketball in the street and cleared the street for the fast oncoming vehicles. Quavo was glad the shooters at least stopped shooting for the kids' sake, but they continued taking shots at him on the very next block. They wanted him bad.

Candler Road wasn't too far, just a few minutes away at the speed he was going, but Quavo couldn't help the feeling that he wouldn't make it as a bullet whizzed past his head and grazed the tip of his ear taking a sizable chunk of flesh with it.

"Aaarrrggghhhh!" he barked savagely as he drowned out the pain and tried to focus on steering the ATV so he wouldn't crash. The blood that spilled down the side of his face was a reminder that shit was real, and just one of those oncoming bullets could quickly end his life.

He wished he was on a dirt bike because he would've been able to lose them easier, but he wasn't, so he had to think fast and find a way. Just when he was beginning to panic as another wave of bullets flew towards him, a pickup truck was approaching the four-way street. The pickup was moving too fast to consider stopping at the stop sign, so that meant he couldn't see Quavo and his company yet, and that was a good thing.

Quavo hit the clutch, and the gas even harder causing him to speed up. The Jeep was about twenty-five feet behind him, and that's all the distance he needed. He shot past the four-way and looked at the driver of the pickup truck, who was about fifteen feet away from the intersection.

Quavo turned around to see that the two trucks didn't crash like he anticipated, but the Jeep did have to stop in order to avoid a collision which gave him a better lead. He was sure to lose them now.

"Ohhhhh!" he spat with wide eyes and an open mouth, after turning back around.

A car was backing out of the driveway of a house on a slight hill. They didn't see Quavo until it was too late and Quavo was going extremely too fast to slow down fast enough, but he still hit the brakes in hopes on stopping the inevitable.

Skurrrr! Boom!

Quavo's four-wheeler slapped the side of the car so hard that it sent him nine feet high into the air and flung him twenty-three feet across the street where he collided headfirst with the concrete floor.

***

Mazi was flying high in the clouds with the birds and planes. He wasn't in a plane and he didn't have a parachute attached to his back. He was literally flying like Superman. The only problem was he didn't know where he was going. It was like he was being guided by a higher power. He was being guided somewhere, and it felt like he needed to be there.

He should've been freezing considering the temperature, high winds, and the fact that he only wore jeans and a short-sleeve T-shirt, but he felt okay. He wasn't worried about that, he just wanted to know where he was being led.

Sunlight was shining above the clouds, but as he descended below them, it was like entering a whole different world completely. It was dark and very hot. Endless pits of fire, and mini volcanoes that erupted repeatedly. He was guided down right into the midst of it all. Just like the cold above, he wasn't affected by the heat below.

What began as distant whistles, became close screeches that got louder and louder as he descended. A train on people came into his eyesight. The line extended as far as his eyes could see. Naked individuals of all shapes, sizes, and ages crawled on their hands and knees at a slap crawl. They maneuvered through the fire pits, and ponds of volcanic lava like a trail of ants on their way home, but this was far from that.

He got down to ground level, but his feet never touched the ground. He was levitating ten feet above the ground, just close enough to see the crawling individuals clearly. He was confused until a familiar face came into his view. He only caught a side view of the face but couldn't place the identity yet.

He tried to get closer but the higher power that was guiding him wouldn't allow it, so he just sat there and waited for the individual to reveal enough of its face for him to identify them. A few short minutes later, his heart dropped. The light-skinned individual was his heart. The one person he loved more than anyone else in the world. Toe-Tag was at least seventy pounds below his usual weight, and his tattoos were barely visible under the burned flesh he wore as skin.

"Lil' bro!" Mazi called out desperately trying to get his little brother's attention, but it was to no avail. Toe-Tag's body was but a shell.

Mazi tried to get to Toe-Tag again. This time with all his might, but he just couldn't. He was forced to watch his brother in pain, and it tore him to pieces. Toe-Tag had tears of blood flowing steadily from his eyes dripping to the ground. Mazi had never seen his brother look so helpless in his life.

"H-h-hhhuuuhhhh!" Mazi woke up from his midday nap gasping for breath. He must've been holding his breath for some time.

His silky polyester Burberry sheets were soaking wet from his sweat, he was drenched in it. He took his hand and ran it down his face and sweat literally dripped from it. He'd never experienced *anything* like it before, and the fact that he remembered the dream vividly made matters even worse. He had to get to his brother.

He didn't even bother to hop in the shower to clean the sweat from his body. He headed straight to the closet and threw on a pair of sweats with his T-shirt before rushed out of the apartment. When he didn't find Toe-Tag in his condo, he began to panic. He'd tried calling his phone before he left his apartment, but it kept going straight to voicemail. After calling Shanay with no luck, he felt it in the pit of his stomach that something wasn't right.

He rushed out of the condo and descended the stairs. He spotted a young group of Mobsters by the green box on the side of Toe-Tag's building and made his way over to them. They seemed to be enjoying themselves until one of them noticed Mazi storming their way like an eighteen-wheeler. "Y'all seen my brother?"

"He just took off about thirty minutes ago. We asked him if he wanted us to come with him, but he said *no*. He needed to be by his self," one of them informed.

"Dammnnn!" Mazi barked making three out of four of them jump.

He walked away with both hands on his head frustration. His eyes were shut tight trying his best to think where Toe-Tag would've gone by himself. He could only think of one place, and it was worth the try. He hopped in his car and swerved off on a mission.

Ten minutes later, he was parking in front of Sky Haven Elementary. There were still a few cars in the parking lot, but it was after school hours so there weren't too many people out. Mazi hopped out of his car and walked off the premises across the street into the woods careful that he wasn't seen. He followed the trail and found exactly what he was looking for. Toe-Tag laid on his back on top of a small blanket with his feet hanging off the edges of the drop that he was so obsessed with.

Mazi stopped in his tracks and looked at his brother worriedly. He raised Toe-Tag and knew him better than anybody else. He knew that his little brother was doing good in a sense, but he was struggling with his mental health. Nobody else noticed, but he could see the effort Toe-Tag put in to fight insanity. It was amazing to him. He never admitted it, but he looked up to Toe-Tag, and that was saying *a lot*.

"What I tell you about wandering around by yourself? You know niggas want your head. Plus, it's a war going on right now," Mazi stated.

Toe-Tag didn't say a word, so Mazi moved closer, and learned that Toe-Tag had headphones in both ears with music blasting. His mood switched from concern to anger less than a second. He kicked Toe-Tag on the shoulder making him jump up with wide eyes.

Toe-Tag removed the headphones out of his ears. "What the hell you doing out here?"

"Nigga, I'm supposed to be asking you the same shit. Why the fuck you out here lacking like this? Listening to music with your eyes closed? Let me find out you giving up, shawty," Mazi spat sternly with disappointment dripping from every word.

Toe-Tag sat up and sighed deeply without saying a word. He just sat there shaking his head slowly.

Mazi kneeled with slight effort and took a seat next to his brother. "Wassam, lil' nigga? Talk to me. I know how you feeling. Monster's death fucking with me, too, but you got too many people depending on you to be out here like this, my nigga," said Mazi.

"The same shit you telling me, right now, just make sure you remember it when it's your time, bro. This crown I'm wearing on my head got a curse on it. We do the Devil's work, and that nigga there don't play fair at all. You do all this shit for him, and he don't do nothing but repay you with a free trip to hell," Toe-Tag philosophized.

Mazi gave him a twisted look. "Man, I hear what you saying, but you got too much going on to be right here worrying about hell. You still on earth, right now, and you got business to handle."

Toe-Tag let out a short burst of psychotic laughter. "Come ride with me real quick. I got a meeting with Kapo."

CHAPTER 40

Mazi followed Toe-Tag back to their hood, Toe-Tag parked his truck and hopped in the car with Mazi. Toe-Tag had a meeting with Kapo, but he showed up late because he had to handle some very important business before they got there.

Kapo called the meeting at a different location this time. The same warehouse that he bought for Toe-Tag. He had the same access as Toe-Tag, so he was already inside waiting by the time Toe-Tag arrived.

"Wait for me out here," Toe-Tag instructed when he saw Mazi reaching for the door handle.

"What? You got me fucked up!" Mazi stated offensively. "I don't know what your problem is? But I'm not letting you go in there by yourself."

"Just chill. The man told me to come in alone, bro. I'll be right back out," Toe-Tag lied in his brother's face before stepping out of the car and making his way into the warehouse.

Kapo's security patted Toe-Tag down at the entrance relieving him of his firearm as usual. Toe-Tag walked into the warehouse and found Kapo staring at Spider's dry blood on the floor. The expression he displayed on his face was just as serious as the tailored suit he wore. "I got word how you had him whacked. What's that all about?"

Toe-Tag didn't answer right away as he walked further into the warehouse towards Kapo. They shared a weird relationship. Even weirder than the one that Rampage had with Kapo. Rampage looked up to Kapo and respected him, but with Toe-Tag shit was very different. He only fucked with Kapo because he saw opportunity.

"He really would've died quick any other time, but that situation was delicate," Toe-Tag explained.

Kapo looked up at him with a questionable expression. "Delicate how?"

"It really wasn't for Spider. I mean, he was gon' get whacked either way, but the way he died wasn't punishment for him. It was punishment for one of my Mobsters. The lil' nigga that did it."

"Ohhhhh, okay," Kapo said understandably. "I know what you mean. Why you didn't spare Spider, though? You know it wasn't him that went against your orders."

Toe-Tag gave him a knowing look. "You know how this shit goes. He responsible for his camp."

"Exactlyyy! Every made-man is responsible for their camps. That's the golden rule for Dilluminati, but exceptions could've been made for Spider like they were made for you," said Kapo.

"What the hell you talking about?" Toe-Tag asked in confusion.

"Naturally, I was supposed to have you whacked after the war with the crips, but I spared you, just like you could've spared Spider," Kapo stated matter-of-factly.

Toe-Tag flashed an unpredictable smile at Kapo. It was genuine. He was really amused. "You ain't too good at this I see."

"What?"

"Being the last voice somebody hears before they die. You know that dramatic speech somebody give before they have the next nigga killed. I been doing this shit, Kapo. I know the game by now. I fucked up, and it's my turn to disappear," Toe-Tag informed accurately.

Kapo was thrown off by Toe-Tag's statement. That was the last thing he expected. He'd never seen someone so comfortable with the threat of death. Not even Rampage, and that was saying a lot. "So, you do understand why I called this meeting at the warehouse instead of my office?"

"Come on, Kap'. Like I said, I'm not new to the game no more. It's just my time, that's all. I got one request, though."

Kapo was thrown for another loop by the request. "Request?"

"Yeah, nigga. You heard me."

"What is it?"

Toe-Tag looked back at Glock and Bullet, who were standing only a few feet behind him. "Make sure my brother takes my spot. He's not dumb enough to do it straight up, or even right away, but he will try to whack you eventually so I advise you to keep your distance."

Kapo nodded. "It's a deal," he said before giving Glock a knowing look.

Pssst! Glock put a single silenced bullet into the back of Toe-Tag's head ending his reign of terror forever.

THE END

FOR NOW!

Submission Guideline

Submit the first three chapters of your completed manuscript to ldpsubmissions@gmail.com, subject line: Your book's title. The manuscript must be in a .doc file and sent as an attachment. Document should be in Times New Roman, double spaced and in size 12 font. Also, provide your synopsis and full contact information. If sending multiple submissions, they must each be in a separate email.

Have a story but no way to send it electronically? You can still submit to LDP/Ca$h Presents. Send in the first three chapters, written or typed, of your completed manuscript to:

LDP: Submissions Dept
Po Box 944
Stockbridge, Ga 30281

DO NOT send original manuscript. Must be a duplicate.

Provide your synopsis and a cover letter containing your full contact information.

Thanks for considering LDP and Ca$h Presents.

BOW DOWN TO MY GANGSTA

By **Ca$h**

TORN BETWEEN TWO

By **Coffee**

THE STREETS STAINED MY SOUL **II**

By **Marcellus Allen**

BLOOD OF A BOSS **VI**

SHADOWS OF THE GAME II

By **Askari**

LOYAL TO THE GAME **IV**

By **T.J. & Jelissa**

A DOPEBOY'S PRAYER **II**

By **Eddie "Wolf" Lee**

IF LOVING YOU IS WRONG… **III**

By **Jelissa**

TRUE SAVAGE **VII**

MIDNIGHT CARTEL III

DOPE BOY MAGIC IV

By **Chris Green**

BLAST FOR ME **III**

A SAVAGE DOPEBOY III

CUTTHROAT MAFIA II

By **Ghost**

A HUSTLER'S DECEIT III

KILL ZONE **II**

BAE BELONGS TO ME III

A DOPE BOY'S QUEEN II

By **Aryanna**

Malik D. Rice

CHAINED TO THE STREETS III
By **J-Blunt**
COKE KINGS V
KING OF THE TRAP II
By **T.J. Edwards**
GORILLAZ IN THE BAY V
De'Kari
THE STREETS ARE CALLING II
Duquie Wilson
KINGPIN KILLAZ IV
STREET KINGS III
PAID IN BLOOD III
CARTEL KILLAZ IV
DOPE GODS II
Hood Rich
SINS OF A HUSTLA II
ASAD
TRIGGADALE III
Elijah R. Freeman
KINGZ OF THE GAME V
Playa Ray
SLAUGHTER GANG IV
RUTHLESS HEART IV
By Willie Slaughter
THE HEART OF A SAVAGE III
By Jibril Williams
FUK SHYT II
By Blakk Diamond
FEAR MY GANGSTA 5
THE REALEST KILLAS

186

New to the Game 3

By Tranay Adams
TRAP GOD II
By Troublesome
YAYO IV
A SHOOTER'S AMBITION III
By S. Allen
GHOST MOB
Stilloan Robinson
KINGPIN DREAMS III
By Paper Boi Rari
CREAM
By Yolanda Moore
SON OF A DOPE FIEND II
By Renta
FOREVER GANGSTA II
GLOCKS ON SATIN SHEETS II
By Adrian Dulan
LOYALTY AIN'T PROMISED II
By Keith Williams
THE PRICE YOU PAY FOR LOVE II
DOPE GIRL MAGIC III
By Destiny Skai
CONFESSIONS OF A GANGSTA II
By Nicholas Lock
I'M NOTHING WITHOUT HIS LOVE II
By Monet Dragun
CAUGHT UP IN THE LIFE III
By Robert Baptiste
LIFE OF A SAVAGE IV
A GANGSTA'S QUR'AN II

By **Romell Tukes**

QUIET MONEY II

By **Trai'Quan**

THE STREETS MADE ME II

By **Larry D. Wright**

THE ULTIMATE SACRIFICE VI

IF YOU CROSSM ME ONCE II

By **Anthony Fields**

THE LIFE OF A HOOD STAR

By Ca\$h & Rashia Wilson

Available Now

RESTRAINING ORDER **I & II**

By **CA\$H & Coffee**

LOVE KNOWS NO BOUNDARIES **I II & III**

By **Coffee**

RAISED AS A GOON I, II, III & IV

BRED BY THE SLUMS I, II, III

BLAST FOR ME I & II

ROTTEN TO THE CORE I II III

A BRONX TALE I, II, III

DUFFEL BAG CARTEL I II III IV

HEARTLESS GOON I II III IV

A SAVAGE DOPEBOY I II

HEARTLESS GOON I II III

DRUG LORDS I II III

CUTTHROAT MAFIA

New to the Game 3

By **Ghost**
LAY IT DOWN **I & II**
LAST OF A DYING BREED
BLOOD STAINS OF A SHOTTA I & II III
By **Jamaica**
LOYAL TO THE GAME I II III
LIFE OF SIN I, II III
By **TJ & Jelissa**
BLOODY COMMAS I & II
SKI MASK CARTEL I II & III
KING OF NEW YORK I II,III IV V
RISE TO POWER I II III
COKE KINGS I II III IV
BORN HEARTLESS I II III IV
KING OF THE TRAP
By **T.J. Edwards**
IF LOVING HIM IS WRONG…I & II
LOVE ME EVEN WHEN IT HURTS I II III
By **Jelissa**
WHEN THE STREETS CLAP BACK I & II III
THE HEART OF A SAVAGE I II
By **Jibril Williams**
A DISTINGUISHED THUG STOLE MY HEART I II & III
LOVE SHOULDN'T HURT I II III IV
RENEGADE BOYS I II III IV
PAID IN KARMA I II III
By **Meesha**
A GANGSTER'S CODE I &, II III
A GANGSTER'S SYN I II III
THE SAVAGE LIFE I II III

CHAINED TO THE STREETS I II
By J-Blunt
PUSH IT TO THE LIMIT
By **Bre' Hayes**
BLOOD OF A BOSS **I, II, III, IV, V**
SHADOWS OF THE GAME
By **Askari**
THE STREETS BLEED MURDER **I, II & III**
THE HEART OF A GANGSTA I II& III
By **Jerry Jackson**
CUM FOR ME I II III IV V
An **LDP Erotica Collaboration**
BRIDE OF A HUSTLA **I II & II**
THE FETTI GIRLS **I, II& III**
CORRUPTED BY A GANGSTA I, II III, IV
BLINDED BY HIS LOVE
THE PRICE YOU PAY FOR LOVE
DOPE GIRL MAGIC I II
By **Destiny Skai**
WHEN A GOOD GIRL GOES BAD
By **Adrienne**
THE COST OF LOYALTY I II III
By Kweli
A GANGSTER'S REVENGE **I II III & IV**
THE BOSS MAN'S DAUGHTERS I II III IV V
A SAVAGE LOVE **I & II**
BAE BELONGS TO ME I II
A HUSTLER'S DECEIT I, II, III
WHAT BAD BITCHES DO I, II, III
SOUL OF A MONSTER I II III

KILL ZONE
A DOPE BOY'S QUEEN
By **Aryanna**
A KINGPIN'S AMBITON
A KINGPIN'S AMBITION **II**
I MURDER FOR THE DOUGH
By **Ambitious**
TRUE SAVAGE I II III IV V VI
DOPE BOY MAGIC I, II, III
MIDNIGHT CARTEL I II
By **Chris Green**
A DOPEBOY'S PRAYER
By **Eddie "Wolf" Lee**
THE KING CARTEL **I, II & III**
By **Frank Gresham**
THESE NIGGAS AIN'T LOYAL **I, II & III**
By **Nikki Tee**
GANGSTA SHYT **I II &III**
By **CATO**
THE ULTIMATE BETRAYAL
By **Phoenix**
BOSS'N UP **I , II & III**
By **Royal Nicole**
I LOVE YOU TO DEATH
By Destiny J
I RIDE FOR MY HITTA
I STILL RIDE FOR MY HITTA
By **Misty Holt**
LOVE & CHASIN' PAPER
By **Qay Crockett**

Malik D. Rice

TO DIE IN VAIN
SINS OF A HUSTLA
By **ASAD**
BROOKLYN HUSTLAZ
By **Boogsy Morina**
BROOKLYN ON LOCK I & II
By **Sonovia**
GANGSTA CITY
By **Teddy Duke**
A DRUG KING AND HIS DIAMOND I & II III
A DOPEMAN'S RICHES
HER MAN, MINE'S TOO I, II
CASH MONEY HO'S
By Nicole Goosby
TRAPHOUSE KING **I II & III**
KINGPIN KILLAZ I II III
STREET KINGS I II
PAID IN BLOOD **I II**
CARTEL KILLAZ I II III
DOPE GODS
By **Hood Rich**
LIPSTICK KILLAH **I, II, III**
CRIME OF PASSION I II & III
By **Mimi**
STEADY MOBBN' **I, II, III**
THE STREETS STAINED MY SOUL
By **Marcellus Allen**
WHO SHOT YA **I, II, III**
SON OF A DOPE FIEND
Renta

GORILLAZ IN THE BAY **I II III IV**

TEARS OF A GANGSTA I II

DE'KARI

TRIGGADALE I II

Elijah R. Freeman

GOD BLESS THE TRAPPERS I, II, III

THESE SCANDALOUS STREETS I, II, III

FEAR MY GANGSTA I, II, III IV

THESE STREETS DON'T LOVE NOBODY I, II

BURY ME A G I, II, III, IV, V

A GANGSTA'S EMPIRE I, II, III, IV

THE DOPEMAN'S BODYGAURD I II

Tranay Adams

THE STREETS ARE CALLING

Duquie Wilson

MARRIED TO A BOSS… I II III

By Destiny Skai & Chris Green

KINGZ OF THE GAME I II III IV

Playa Ray

SLAUGHTER GANG I II III

RUTHLESS HEART I II III

By Willie Slaughter

FUK SHYT

By Blakk Diamond

DON'T F#CK WITH MY HEART I II

By Linnea

ADDICTED TO THE DRAMA I II III

By Jamila

YAYO I II III

A SHOOTER'S AMBITION I II

By S. Allen
TRAP GOD
By Troublesome
FOREVER GANGSTA
GLOCKS ON SATIN SHEETS
By Adrian Dulan
TOE TAGZ I II III
By Ah'Million
KINGPIN DREAMS I II
By Paper Boi Rari
CONFESSIONS OF A GANGSTA
By Nicholas Lock
I'M NOTHING WITHOUT HIS LOVE
By Monet Dragun
CAUGHT UP IN THE LIFE I II
By Robert Baptiste
NEW TO THE GAME I II III
By **Malik D. Rice**
LIFE OF A SAVAGE I II III
A GANGSTA'S QUR'AN
By **Romell Tukes**
LOYALTY AIN'T PROMISED
By Keith Williams
Quiet Money
By **Trai'Quan**
THE STREETS MADE ME
By **Larry D. Wright**
THE ULTIMATE SACRIFICE I, II, III, IV, V
KHADIFI
IF YOU CROSS ME ONCE

By **Anthony Fields**

THE LIFE OF A HOOD STAR

By Ca$h & Rashia Wilson

Malik D. Rice

BOOKS BY LDP'S CEO, CA$H

TRUST IN NO MAN

TRUST IN NO MAN 2

TRUST IN NO MAN 3

BONDED BY BLOOD

SHORTY GOT A THUG

THUGS CRY

THUGS CRY 2

THUGS CRY 3

TRUST NO BITCH

TRUST NO BITCH 2

TRUST NO BITCH 3

TIL MY CASKET DROPS

RESTRAINING ORDER

RESTRAINING ORDER 2

IN LOVE WITH A CONVICT

LIFE OF A HOOD STAR

Coming Soon

BONDED BY BLOOD 2

BOW DOWN TO MY GANGSTA

New to the Game 3

www.ingramcontent.com/pod-product-compliance
Lightning Source LLC
Chambersburg PA
CBHW070019260626
47159CB00005B/1874